September 29, 1982

CALLING HOME

For Aharon Empey

New stories by

MERNA SUMMERS

Some of us have class, and some of us have classmates! Best wishes—Merna Summers

Acknowledgments: "Calling Home" first appeared in *Matrix*. "City Wedding" was broadcast on CBC's *Anthology*. "Hooking Things" was first published in *Dandelion*; "Threshing Time" originally appeared in *Nimrod*, and won the Katherine Anne Porter prize for fiction, awarded jointly by *Nimrod* and the University of Tulsa.

ISBN 0 88750 448 5 (hardcover)
ISBN 0 88750 449 3 (softcover)

Cover by Jean Richards
Book design by Michael Macklem

Printed in Canada

PUBLISHED IN CANADA BY OBERON PRESS

For Melva

RONNIE SO LONG AT THE FAIR

There was absolutely no reason to smoke that he could think of, but it seemed that he was determined to do it. He lay on his bed, his cigarette on a jam-can lid beside him, and watched the smoke rise and form a layer between bed and ceiling. He was seventeen, past the age where he ought to have done such things, and he didn't want to be a laggard at the table of life.

So he was thinking, and congratulating himself for procrastinating no longer, when he heard the voices at the back door. He leapt from his bed, he who had thought that the only way he could get up was very, very slowly, and picked up a dirty shirt and began to fan it toward the window. Before the voices he had had one problem; now he had two.

"It's not worth it," he said to himself, meaning the smoking. "I'm going to give it up."

The truth was that he was having a hard time getting it started, that smoking made him dizzy, that he had to take to his bed to do it. But he was practising, and it seemed to him that he was making progress. He might have finished this cigarette if his mother hadn't come home. He had smoked two-thirds of it already and he still had some smoking capacity left.

The voices in the kitchen reached him over the sound of his shirt flapping. His mother's voice, complacent. "We *do* get along pretty well." And Mrs. Warner's, congratulating, flattering. "I should think you do. There's a lot of mothers would envy you."

He realized that they were talking about him, registered the fact without much interest. Then his mother spoke again. "When Ronnie was just a little fellow he used to say, 'You're my best friend, Mum.'"

Hearing this, Ron felt his skin move over his body as if it were trying to dissociate itself from the rest of him. Mostly, as his mother said, they did get along pretty well...but he wished she would stop telling people things he had said when he was a little kid. And he wished she would stop calling him *Ronnie.*

He dribbled some Kool-Aid on top of the cigarette butt in the jam-can lid and then poured the whole mess out of the window into the petunia bed. His clothes would smell of smoke, he realized. He had to go through the kitchen to get out of the house and his mother and Mrs. Warner would smell him.

Let them smell him, he thought. He was old enough to do

6

as he pleased. There wasn't a thing his mother could say to him.

But when he was dressed and ready to go it seemed to him that there was no point in making a big thing of it and so he made a run for it, speeding through the kitchen and calling "Sorry, I'm late" over his shoulder. Then he was outside and one problem was behind him.

What was ahead of him wasn't exactly a problem but a party...which amounted to the same thing, Ron thought. He was going to a party. He didn't expect very much of it. He didn't expect very much of any of the parties he went to.

Parties in Willow Bunch never seemed like *real* parties. They seemed like poor makeshifts, like imitations of the kind of parties that people would have in other places. He wouldn't have gone to them at all if he hadn't needed the practice, and felt that the practice you got at imitation parties was better than no practice at all.

One of the things he needed practice with was girls; he didn't know how to get started with them. It seemed to him that if he could get started he would know how to carry on, but he didn't kow how to get started. It was one of the things he would have liked to ask his father about, if he had had a father to ask, but his father hadn't come home from the war.

That was the way they always said it: that his father hadn't come home from the war. It was the phrase that was used for men who had been killed overseas, but his father hadn't been killed overseas. He had simply decided not to come back to Willow Bunch when the war was over.

"He's tom-catting around somewhere in England," Ron had overheard his mother telling Mrs. Warner. "Well, good luck to him. I'm sure I wouldn't want to hold him back."

His mother hadn't sounded bitter or unhappy. She had a light girlish voice and she spoke briskly, as one disposing of an inconvenient fact, putting it in its place. And Ron, who was twelve then, had not known what tom-catting meant.

He had thought that it must be the code word for some kind of secret mission. He had imagined his father coming home when the mission was over, had imagined how impressed people would be. Platforms would be decorated and medals presented, he had thought. "Sappy kid," he thought now, remembering. But the memory made him uncomfortable, as if it were not a thing that he had thought long ago, but recently.

He was supposed to call on Preston Blackwell, but Preston was waiting for him in the lane, his portable record-player in his hand. "Christ we're late," he said as Ron came up.

"I'm in no hurry," Ron said.

They walked along together in silence for a while. Then, "Do you think there'll be any new girls at the party?" Preston asked.

Ron had already considered this. If it were two weeks later and the summer holidays, some of the girls might have had cousins or pen-pals staying with them, and brought them to the party. But the last week of school?

"Not much chance," he said.

He began then to think of the girls who *would* be at the party—Lorraine Fenske, Shirley Larson, Derry Drake—and it was as if each of them had a question mark behind her name. He always thought of girls that way: as if they had question marks behind their names. One of them was going to mean something to him, he thought, but he had no way of knowing which one that was going to be.

They turned a corner and came into sight of the church hall, where the party was being held, and Ron felt a sudden reluctance to go any farther. "Shall we stop for a smoke?" he asked.

Preston looked impatient. "Can't you wait?" he said. "We're late now."

Ron shrugged. "I guess I can sneak out later," he said.

8

There were as many boys as girls at the party, but the room seemed to be full of girls. They fluttered around in their light summer dresses, twice as noticeable as boys; you couldn't not notice them. The way they dressed, the perfume they wore, the way they talked: all these things were meant for noticing. Beside them the boys seemed colourless, smell-less, sound-less. It seemed to Ron that even a girl would have a hard time finding anything about most of them to be interested in.

Preston took his record-player up to the front and busied himself with setting it up, and Ron went to stand beside Walter Hafner, a farm boy he chummed with when he was on Uncle Ross's farm. "I wondered if you'd changed your mind about coming," Walter said.

Ron nodded, acknowledging the possibility. "There was nothing else to do," he said. "There never is in this burg."

He felt better when he had said that, as if he had put himself on top of the situation.

The girls were talking in voices higher than they needed to be heard. They were standing in a group at the other side of the hall, but the centre of their group was not a girl and he was not standing. Alf Henderson, older than the rest of them and working now, was sprawled on a seat, almost sitting on his spine, drooping his eyelids as if to say that it was going to take something pretty special to interest him. As far as Ron could see, Alf behaved in exactly the way his mother had taught him that you didn't behave around girls, but the girls clustered around him as if he were candy. Which went to show that you couldn't believe everything that you were taught, Ron thought, that if there was anything useful to be learned, you were going to learn it from your own generation.

Walter was watching too. "Dames," he said with disgust.

"Yeah," Ron said.

After a while Alf stood up, and there was a blatant male-ness about the way he did it. He hoisted himself from the

9

belt, the way Ron had seen truck drivers in the coffee shop do when they stood up.

"Look at him," Walter said. "Lifting his nuts. He's got to make sure they're still there."

"Yeah," Ron said.

Ron hadn't expected much of the party, but afterwards it seemed to him that he had got more than he expected, and that this party was more real than other parties he had been to. What made this party different was that he went out on the porch for air with a girl. He was dancing with Derry Drake, and it was hot, and when the dance ended, Derry suggested that they go out for air.

Ron was glad that it was Derry who asked him. Derry wasn't the prettiest girl at the party—Derry's face wasn't really *pretty* —but she was perhaps the most striking. Blond hair always drew your eyes to a girl, and Derry's hair was so blonde that it was almost silver. Besides that, there was an air of imminent happenings about Derry. She leaned forward when she talked, as if she couldn't wait to get where she was going, and you felt that her life had more excitement in it than most people's. Derry's father was a lawyer and Ron was impressed by this, although he didn't know why he should be.

On the porch Ron reached into his pocket and took out his pack of Exports. "Smoke?" he asked.

Derry shook her head. "I would, but I don't like the smell," she said. "You go ahead, though."

Ron put the cigarettes away. "Actually, I'm trying to quit," he said.

After that Ron didn't know what to do, but Derry asked him what he was doing in the summer holidays and he told her that he always worked for Uncle Ross and it seemed to him that she looked at him with admiration. Then she asked if he was going to the Vermilion Fair and he said he was thinking about it and she said, "Maybe I'll see you there, then."

It wasn't a date, Ron told himself later, you couldn't call it a date. But still, *something* had happened. He only wished that he had thought to ask Derry what day she was going to the fair.

The water in the wash-basin was almost mud. Ron grinned, pleased that all this dirt had come off his face and hands. On the farm he did a man's work and he felt like a man. Stacking bales or driving the big Minnie, he was conscious of power, his own and the machine's. Of its own accord his body took on a man's way of moving, a way of moving that took up space, too much space for his mother's little house in town.

'I thought you were going to take a bath," Uncle Ross said as Ron dumped the dirty water and filled the wash-basin again.

"I am," Ron said. "I'm just taking the rough off. I don't want to get my bath water dirty."

Uncle Ross whistled. "It sounds like a heavy date," he said.

Ron grinned again. He was going to the fair with Walter, but he and Walter *might* pick up a couple of girls, he thought. They might see Derry and one of her friends, and tie up with them, or they might meet some new girls. He had a strong feeling of possibility. There were times when he felt inspired with knowledge about how to act with girls, and today had been one of those days.

This feeling increased as he and Walter drove across country to the fair. It was early evening, and summer was at its height, and it seemed to him that the world itself was giving him messages about how to conduct his affairs. He looked at the fenceposts sending shadows across the wheat and barley fields, shadows long in the long light of evening, and he listened to the song of a meadowlark rising from fencepost to sky. *Reach,* these things said to him. And he breathed in the scent of newly made hay, of purple clover blooming in the ditches, and felt himself instructed by their fragrance. *Touch* was what they told him.

They parked the car on the road outside the fairgrounds. Ahead they could see the Rollo-plane circling and diving, the Ferris wheel drawing circles of light against a still-bright sky, and Ron's feeling that this was the night, that something was going to happen, grew. The fair was a different world, a world where the ordinary rules didn't apply. You might not know how to get started other places, but here you would know how to get started.

Ron and Walter passed through the Exhibits Building quickly. Other people might come to the fair to look at the winter wheat and the red currant jelly, but they weren't among them. They spared not a glance for the vibrating chairs or, outside, the avenues of green farm machinery. They did stop for a minute to look at a Holstein cow standing in a pen under a striped canopy. *Alcartra Gerben, The World's Champion Milk Producer*, a sign in front of the cow said, and seeing it, Ron felt a stir of pride, of confirmation. The Vermilion Fair might only be a little C Circuit fair, he thought, but it had managed to get a World's Champion here. That must mean something.

Then they were on to the Midway, with its smell of frying onions, its booths of kewpie dolls in feather skirts, its plumed hats with bands that said *Hubba Hubba*. This was the heart of the fair, and Ron felt as if he had come to a place of testing. That was what the fair was, he thought: a kind of test. You could test your skill, or your luck, or your stength. And what else were the rides but a kind of test? You went on the wild ones the first time to see if you could take it. And afterwards you felt more of a man for it.

There was a concession where people shot ducks on a moving belt. The girl who ran the concession was about Ron's age, but she had a tattoo on each bare shoulder. Ron was looking at her, thinking that she looked as if she would be interesting to talk to, when he heard a little squeal and turned to see where it had come from. Then he saw the girls —Derry Drake and Lorraine Fenske—and he wondered why he hadn't seen them sooner. They were dressed to stand out in a crowd, Derry especially. She had on white slacks and a paddy-green blouse, and a crazy hat with a long plume on it. She looked like a tap-dancer, or like somebody who might belong to the fair.

Walter saw the girls too. He didn't say anything, just motioned in their direction with his head. And as he and Ron moved forward together Derry turned and Ron saw that she had seen them first and was checking to make sure that they had seen her.

Ron hadn't seen Derry since school ended. He had thought about her, had made stories about her and himself, as he sometimes made stories about his father and himself. He didn't know very much about either of them, outside of the way they were in his stories, but it seemed to him that if you imagined a person a certain way, they probably were like that. But at the same time, he knew that Derry was the girl in his stories because she was the girl he had gone out on the porch with; if something had happened with another girl, he would have thought about her instead.

"Well, look who's here," Derry said.

"This is your lucky day," Walter said.

They stood around for a while then, joking, and then Ron said, "I guess we might as well take a stroll around and see what there is to see," including the girls in the invitation. He felt expansive saying it, liked the way it sounded coming out.

They set off paired, Walter with Lorraine and Ron with Derry, and with Ron thinking about the commands he had been getting about reaching and touching. There was a poem in a book at school about young people at a fair, seeking out the bypaths and kissing bridges. It occurred to Ron that the

Vermilion Fair was a little short of both. If he wanted to touch Derry he was going to have to reach out right in the middle of the Midway, where the whole world could see if she moved away.

But then he thought of the rides. The rides could have been invented for this. On the Tilt-A-Whirl or the Loop-O-Plane, touching would be all but inevitable; centrifugal force would be on your side.

He felt pleased with himself for having thought of this, and pleased when the rides turned out to have precisely the advantages he had foreseen. On the Tilt-A-Whirl, Derry's small body leaned against him and his leaned against her. On the Silver Streak he discovered that the only way two could sit comfortably in the narrow seat was for him to put his arm around her. And by the time they got to the Ferris wheel, to the top of it, he felt able to kiss her, and did, but not very well. It wasn't that their noses collided or anything like that, but he felt as if he wanted to kiss her in a place that wasn't high and swinging, at a time when they didn't have a sickening lurch down ahead of them. He wanted to be able to concentrate.

Immediately he began to think of Walter's car, of how, if they could get to it, they could kiss there.

Walter must have been thinking of the same thing. When they got off the Ferris wheel he said he was hungry, suggested a hamburger. But he said that he wanted to go to the Exhibits Building to get it, that they made better hamburgers there.

Ron was full of admiration. When you were at the Exhibits Building you were half-way to the car. And when their hamburgers were eaten Walter remembered that he had left his sweater in the car and they all set out with him to get it, walking purposefully through the darkness, the Midway lights behind them reflected in the hoods of parked cars.

They got to Walter's car and Walter and Lorraine got in the front and Ron and Derry got in the back. Ron's excitement now was intense. He didn't have time to wonder if he would know how to get started touching Derry. As soon as they got in the car he was doing it. Derry was there, in the handiest place for kissing, and he kissed her. And you couldn't very well sit kissing a girl as if she was nothing but a pair of lips and so he held her.

He didn't expect more than that: a kiss, a touch. It hadn't occurred to him that there could be more. He was not, for instance, expecting to touch anything so personal as a breast. But it somehow happened that Derry's breast was against his hand, and the feeling of it there, soft and warm and thrusting, was almost too much for him. He groaned, heard himself groan.

"Easy back there," Walter said.

Ron remembered then that they were not alone, and took his hand away. But as soon as he had done it, he felt its exile, wanted it back. He was trying to figure out a way of getting it back there without Derry noticing when he realized that he had another problem: Derry was mad at him. She pulled away from him, turning her head, as if he had done something.

He didn't know what to do. After a minute he put out a hand and touched Derry tentatively, and it seemed to him that Derry moved back a little, that she was not quite as far away as she had been. He kissed the back of her neck, which was the part of her that was closest to him, and then it was as if Derry forgave him for whatever he had done because she turned and began to kiss him urgently, her breasts pressing against his chest. It seemed to Ron that this was an accident, but he accepted it gratefully. Derry must not feel things like he did, he thought. It occurred to him that he liked everything about Derry, but that this absent-mindedness of hers was the best thing of all. He betted he could touch her all over and she wouldn't notice at all.

The thought made him feel like groaning again, but this time he did not groan. He was learning, he thought, and at a rate he would not have believed possible.

All the time he was thinking these things he was kissing away like crazy. It seemed to him astonishing the way he could think and do at once, that the harder he kissed the faster he thought, and the more daring his thoughts became. He decided to try putting his hand on Derry's breast again, and it was just as he thought: she didn't notice it there at all, but just kissed him harder than before. He thought of how much there was of Derry that might be touched, and goodness knows what part of him or of her might have got into the touching next if Lorraine hadn't spoken from the front seat. "My God," she said. "It's 11. I'm going to get killed."

It turned out that Derry and Lorraine had come to the fair with Lorraine's parents, and had to go home with them. But Derry didn't move away from him, didn't shrug his hand off her breast, until Lorraine opened the front door and the car light came on. Then his hand dropped of its own accord.

They walked the girls back to the Midway. Later, walking back to the car, "How did you make out?" Walter asked. And then, not waiting for an answer, "You know that little short blouse that Lorraine was wearing? Well, I had my hand on the skin at her waist."

Ron felt like laughing. "Kid stuff," he could have said. But he wouldn't say it, because then Walter would know how far he had gone with Derry, and he didn't want Walter to know. He realized that now when he dreamed, it would always be about Derry. And he wanted to protect her, he felt that she needed his protection. Because if she had known what was happening, it wouldn't have.

There were two main smells in the kitchen. There was the smell of Uncle Ross's Sunday morning coffee, laced with rum, and there was the smell of chicken gravy, rising from a roaster on top of the stove. His mother was stirring the gravy, if stirring was the right word for what she was doing. Lumps had formed in it and she was attacking them, threshing against them with the back of her spoon. She looked angry.

Ron and his mother had been to church. Ron seldom went in the summertime—it was one of the masculine privileges of being part of Uncle Ross' bachelor establishment that nobody expected you to—and his mother had been surprised when he had turned up this time. He hadn't told her his reason: that Derry was arranging the flowers for the service, that Derry was, she said, "very interested in flower-arranging."

Sitting beside his mother, Ron had thought that the flowers looked fine. But they must not have looked that way to Derry, because just before the service started, she got up and went into the sanctuary to make some last-minute adjustments, moving a snapdragon here, a bachelor button there. She made a pretty picture doing it, with her hair so blond that it was almost silver, and her eyes as blue as the blue skies over Uncle Ross's hayfield. Ron thought that you could look at a blue wall or a blue dress and it didn't do the same thing to you as a blue sky did, but Derry's eyes were different. He felt the same soaring of spirit looking at them as he did looking at a sky.

Derry finished her adjusting and returned to the middle of the altar. She stopped there and bowed deeply, reverently, and there was a look of purity about her. Unbidden, there came into Ron's mind a picture of himself and Derry, years hence, sitting together in this same church. He did not want to get married, he knew that it was years too soon for him to think about getting married, but the picture that formed in his mind was a *married* picture. He saw himself and Derry going home from church for Sunday dinner with "the folks," Derry's parents, Mr. and Mrs. Drake. He saw the white damask on the table, saw Mr. Drake standing at the end of it, carving the roast. That was the way things would be done in the Drake household, he thought: white linen and the carving done at the table.

Derry turned to rejoin her parents in their pew and as she did so, Ron could tell that her eyes were going to move toward the pew where he was sitting with his mother, and they did. But it was not his eyes that Derry sought out, but his mother's.

Ron's mother gave up on her gravy and got out a strainer and grimly began to push it through. Watching her, Ron had the feeling that there was something that he ought to make up to her, but he didn't know what it was. And he wondered how he was going to tell her that he was practically going with Derry Drake, wondered if he had to tell her, or if he could just wait and let her hear about it from somebody else.

But as they sat down to dinner, "What was Derry Drake doing parading around the sanctuary before the service started?" his mother demanded.

Ron answered stiffly. "She was arranging the flowers. She's very interested in flower-arrangement," he said.

"Is that what she calls it?" his mother said. "*Flower-arrangement?*"

The way she said it made Derry sound pretentious, but before Ron could think of a way to reply Uncle Ross had spoken. "Watch it, Wilma," he said. "I think somebody's got a sweetie."

"Ron?" his mother said, and her face grew red. "I should hope that Ron has better things to do with his time than go mooning around over some little *flower-arranger.*"

"Derry and I are going to the ballgame this afternoon," Ron said. "Uncle Ross said I could borrow the truck."

"Really, Ross," his mother said.

But Uncle Ross returned her gaze calmly. "Most natural thing in the world, a boy taking out a girl. You'd better get used to it, Wilma," he said.

For a moment Ron thought that his mother was going to

say something else, but then he could see her struggling to bring herself under control. Finally, "You'll have to excuse me, Ron," she said in her light voice. "Of course you want to take out girls. The more the merrier."

Ron relaxed then. His mother was usually pretty good about things. Once in a while she flew off the handle, but usually she could be persuaded to see things your way. And she had a nice feminine way of apologizing so that whatever the disagreement was, she let you come out of it feeling good.

All that summer, when Ron came to town from the farm, he went to see Derry first and then to see his mother. And often when he came home he was singing a song that he and Derry sang together.

> Honors flysis
> Income beesis
> Onches nobbis
> Innob keesis.

A half-witted girl had sung it in a show they had gone to together, and that song had been the key to the whole movie. You could sing it:

> On horse, flies is
> In comb, bees is
> On chest, knob is
> In knob, keys is.

Only it was more fun to sing it the other way.

The first time his mother heard him sing the song she asked him about it and when he explained it, she said, "It's something like *Hutsa Brolsin on the Rilla Ra.*"

Hutsa Brolsin on the Rilla Ra was a song his mother sometimes sang. It seemed to Ron a silly song, something left over from years ago when his mother was young. "It's not like that at all," he said.

"I guess not," his mother said, but she looked hurt. It occurred to Ron that she was old now, and out of things, and he felt sorry for her.

His mother had apologized after the Sunday that Derry had arranged the flowers, taking all the blame for what had happened on herself and making it clear that she really liked Derry, that if she had been bad-natured it was because there was something else bothering her and she had got the two things mixed up. "I feel sorry for you men," she had said, and given her light little laugh. "Having to put up with poor creatures like us."

And Ron had had to smile. She could charm him, his mother could, but he saw no harm in that. Especially since she had made up her mind to charm Derry too.

"Now you be sure to bring Derry over for cocoa afterwards," she would say whenever she knew that he was taking Derry to the show, and sometimes Ron did that. He had never brought his friends home much. When he was a little kid he had learned that if he had fights, it was best not to let his mother know about them. She took his part too strongly, went to see the principal, or the other boy's mother. And she was almost as bad about his friendships. When boys came to the house she got out all his toys and lined them up, as if to show the boys what they would be missing if they didn't play with him. She baked little cakes and fussed over them and made everyone uncomfortable. But it was different with a girl. Girls liked to be fussed over. "I think your mother's just charming," Derry said, and his mother was. Derry and his mother got along like a house afire.

One night, when he and Derry had been to a musical, "I think that Ron looks just like Dick Haymes," Derry announced when they were back at the house.

Derry didn't think that, Ron knew. She was only trying to

make him feel good.

But his mother took it one step further. "I think that Dick Haymes would be very flattered to hear that," she said. "I think Ron is *much* better looking than Dick Haymes. Don't you?"

And Derry had looked embarrassed, but a minute later she managed to turn the whole thing into a joke. "Now if he could just *sing* like Dick Haymes," she said.

When Derry knew they were coming to see his mother, she would twist her long hair into a bun at the back of her neck and borrow her mother's brown and white spectator pumps to wear. "They just look like your mother," she said when Ron asked her about it.

They didn't. His mother liked clothes that were feminine, not sporty. What they looked like was Derry's idea of the way she should be for his mother, the self that Derry thought was the right one to show. Derry had many selves, Ron was discovering; she changed her *self* the way other people change hats, taking one off and putting another on to see which was more becoming. She would be sedate, a lady, having cocoa with his mother. But then Ron would walk her home and she would either kiss him passionately or else fight with him. It seemed to Ron that whenever he and Derry weren't kissing, they were fighting, and he tried to keep those times as short as possible.

Finding a *place* to kiss was really not a problem, even when the summer holidays ended and he didn't have Uncle Ross' truck any more. The town was full of places you could kiss, dark places where there wasn't somebody going by every five minutes, and it was as if Ron had been filing away information about these places all his life, against the day of need. Most of their kissing, however, was done in Derry's backyard, on the dark side of the Drakes' back porch, because Derry's house was the last place they went every date. Ron would walk Derry home thinking that they weren't going to be doing anything that they couldn't do at her back door, and then, of course, they would do it.

By now Ron knew that Derry was not unaware of what went on when they kissed, that she felt it too. But whenever they were going a little further than they had gone before, she would slip into the same absent-mindedness. And, while Ron didn't really want things to go much further—he wanted to show Derry that he respected her—somehow things always went ahead, they never went back.

At the very first, theirs was an above-the-waist expression of affection. But then somehow Ron understood that anything that he did with his hands was all right. Derry didn't tell him that—they didn't talk about what they were doing, pretended they weren't doing it—but that was what it amounted to.

Ron was grateful. At first he thought that he wanted no more than to feel Derry's body, warm and trusting under his hands. Her body was like a continent and his hands were like two explorers. Here come Lewis and Clark, he thought. Make way for LaVerendrye. Only he really didn't want LaVeredrye getting into it. He had all he could handle now.

But he did, of course. He wanted more. He didn't want everything, but he did want more. When Derry let him touch her *there,* he wanted her to touch him *there.* That was all, he thought, just a touch.

But Derry turned out to be reticent about this. She would let his hand go wherever it wanted to go, do whatever it wanted to do, and sometimes she even showed him the way. But she would not touch him. It was as if what her body did didn't count, because *she* wasn't doing it, but her hand was different. There was a chastity, a purity, about her hand, and Ron respected this. He was almost sick sometimes, respecting it, but he asked for no more than more of the same sickness. Being with Derry could be an agony, and he felt that if he didn't find some way of increasing the agony he would die.

Sometimes he thought that they ought to give the whole thing up. But even if they could have, they couldn't have, because whenever they weren't touching each other, they were fighting. Sometimes Ron would see the telltale signs that Derry intended to pick a fight with him even when they were with his mother. Then he would have to get her away fast to someplace where they could kiss and all the rest it. None of this, of course, was anything that his mother could know or even suspect.

When Ron thought of the future, he thought of it as a time when all the pain would be gone and all the joy left. There would never be any limit to their capacity to feel, he thought, but he and Derry would one day come past the place of hurting. He saw them as together always, and one of the things he wanted was for them to have mementoes of all the stages they had passed through along the way. He thought of Valentine's, when he would give Derry a card a foot high, the kind that comes in a box instead of an envelope, the kind that has a red satin heart and *To My Sweetheart* on it. When he learned that Derry's birthday was in the fall, that he wouldn't have to wait till Valentine's or even Christmas to give her a present, it seemed to him like a great opportunity.

As soon as he saw it, Ron knew that it was what he wanted. The box was shell-shaped, and it was covered with embossed silver paper and lined with pink satin. Inside was a dresser set: a comb, hairbrush, and handmirror, all with pink mother-of-pearl backs. A compact would have done, perfume in an atomizer bottle would have done, but this was perfect. This was a tribute to femininity.

It cost $17, more than he had ever thought of spending on a present for anybody, but he didn't hesitate. And he found it gave him a fine feeling to pull the money out of his pocket to pay for it. You weren't a boy any more when you bought a present like that, he thought; you were a man.

He hadn't intended to show the present to anyone before he gave it to Derry, and if he had remembered to buy wrapping paper for it, he wouldn't have. But when he asked his mother for some wrapping paper and she asked to see it, he couldn't think of any good reason to say no.

"Oh, my," his mother said when she saw it. "Oh, my."

Uncle Ross was there too. "That's some present," he said.

Ron was pleased. "You like it?" he asked.

"You want to watch it, giving presents like that to girls," Uncle Ross said. "They'll be throwing themselves at your head."

But Ron saw that his mother's face had taken on a doubtful look. "You don't think it's a little too much?" she said. And then, "You *know* I want Derry to have a nice present," she said. "You know how much I like Derry. It's just that I'm afraid it's not in good taste for a boy to give a girl a present as elaborate as this."

Ron felt his spirits fall. With a girl like Derry, with parents like hers, taste had to be considered, he felt.

"You do understand that I want Derry to have a nice present, don't you?" his mother said. "It's just that I couldn't bear to have you give her a present so...so..."

"So feminine?" Uncle Ross suggested.

"Yes," his mother said. "I mean no. It's just excessive is all. It's not in good taste."

"What do you think Ron should give her?" Uncle Ross asked.

"Oh, a jigsaw puzzle. A box of handkerchiefs."

Ron almost laughed out loud. A box of handkerchiefs! For a girl like Derry!

His mother saw her mistake. "Well, not a box of handkerchiefs then. But something nice. A bottle of toilet water, maybe. Something that is both nice and in good taste."

Afterwards Ron wondered if his mother might have persuaded him if Uncle Ross hadn't been there. "I don't see very much the matter with this," Uncle Ross said.

Suddenly his mother was angry. "You wouldn't," she said. "You men. You're all alike."

And for no reason at all there came to Ron's mind a parade of presents: the presents he had given to his mother over the years. Fancy bread-boards he had given her, and cushion covers to embroider, and a picture of a moose to hang on the wall. But never a piece of jewellery, never a bottle of perfume. Never a tribute to femininity.

He would make it up to her, he thought.

Then his mother, no longer angry, gave a light, girlish laugh. "Do as you like," she said. "But if Derry doesn't like it, don't say I didn't warn you."

"I'll chance it," Ron said.

As it turned out, Derry did like it. She accepted it with delight, and Ron came to think of the moment he had given it to her as a kind of sacrament they had celebrated together.

It was two weeks later. They were standing on the dark side of her parents' back porch and Derry had her hand inside his pants. It was the first time she had had it there, and it was only tentatively there, as if he were a electric fence that might come on at any minute, as if she might at any minute fly away. By an effort of will Ron kept himself from moving against her. But then, when her hand stayed where it was and then curved around him, he began to move, carefully at first, and then faster. It was unlike anything he had ever experienced before, to do this with someone else, in some ways not quite so good and in other ways a hundred times better.

Afterwards he felt as if there was nothing he could do to show Derry how he felt about her. He would have liked to get down and worship her. He felt that she had proven her love—

realized for the first time that girls *did* prove their love when they did this. They *gave* themselves to you. Bodies that have touched are not like bodies that have not touched. When a thing like this had happened, it couldn't unhappen.

He would never do Derry any harm, he promised himself; he would never do anything that could possibly harm her. But even as he was promising, his mind was going to the thing that he would not do, that he didn't want to do, and the pictures formed in spite of him.

They wouldn't do *that*, he promised himself. But there was something else. He had been sure that if Derry would just touch him *there*, he wouldn't ask for another thing. But now he knew that there was just one more thing he wanted. He wanted to feel his maleness between Derry's legs. Not inside of her, never inside of her until they were older and had some way out of it. Just between her legs. He wanted to feel his *there* against her *there*.

His power had returned to him almost at once and he began to move, putting himself where he wanted to be, and from the way that Derry arranged her body he could tell that she wanted it too. But when he got to where he wanted to be, he stopped. Because when he got there he was half scared of being even this far. It seemed to him that they had gone too far too fast. Maybe another time they would want to go further and then he would have to fight with himself, but for now, he was scared.

Derry began to move and soon he began to move too. But it didn't feel like he wanted it to. Standing like this, they couldn't move enough, and they couldn't move in the right places. Ron's legs began to cramp from the way he had to stand.

Then suddenly Derry moved away from him and Ron saw that for no reason at all she was going to be mad at him. "I wonder what your mother would say if she could see us now," Derry said brutally. "Boy, would I like to see the look on her face."

And Ron recognized that from this end of the evening, with the touching over, there was nothing he could do to make Derry feel better. He cleaned himself up with his hand-kerchief and went home.

He was gone for one weekend and when he came back it was all over. There was absolutely nothing that could have enabled him to predict the breakup.

He went to see Derry, and she came out on the back porch for a minute, but she wouldn't go out with him. "I've got something to tell you," she said.

She told him that her parents didn't think that she should go out with just one boy, and she thought they were right. It was one of the things she had said before, pretending reason, when they were fighting. But Ron knew that while girls in other places might go out with more than one boy at a time, girls here didn't. Here it was off with the old love before you were on with the new. And Derry was his girl.

Then Derry told him that she had gone out with Alf Henderson.

Ron felt as if there was a space of time between the time when Derry told him and the time when he heard it, a time when he could feel its meaning travelling toward him. Derry out with Alf Henderson. He felt there were things that he could not bear to know.

At first he thought that Derry meant to keep on going out with him too, but then he discovered that she did not. What had happened was final, she said. "Some men can make a girl do whatever they want," she whispered. "I'm sorry, Ron."

Ron looked at her, knowing, but unable to comprehend. Just last week when they had been clinging to each other in an anguish of longing, Derry had moaned over and over, "I love you. I love you," and Ron knew that she had meant forever. Now it seemed that she was unable to remember what she had felt then, honestly unable to do it. It was past and she felt it no more. If Ron had reminded her of her feeling she would have denied it and believed that she spoke the truth.

What was a man supposed to do? When a girl liked him one day, couldn't keep her hands off him, and then wanted nothing to do with him the next, what was he supposed to do?

If there had been anything he could have done to get Derry back, Ron would have done it. But he saw that there was nothing. And Derry let him know that there was no question of him overlooking what had happened, made it clear that she would think less of him if he made light of it by accepting it.

There was nothing he could do. Getting mad wouldn't help, and neither would crying. He was powerless. All that Derry asked of him now was that he be on his way, get out of her life. Her voice, which had been sympathetic at the beginning, was already growing impatient, with hard edges in it. He felt that she wanted to laugh, that she wanted to say to him, "Run on home, little boy."

There were no words for the pain he felt as he walked home. He felt a need to be sick, to be in bed, with his mother bringing him things, or to be cut, broken, so that he could be bandaged. He did not tell himself that he should take it like a man. He wasn't sure that he could take it at all. When he got home he crawled into bed, not intending to stay there, but needing a place to hide. But once he was there it was as if his capacity for rising had left him forever. To stand upright, to walk on the earth, seemed like impossibilities.

He did not tell his mother about his breakup with Derry or that Derry was going out with someone else. Instead, three days later, his mother told him.

"Yeah," he said, confirming it. He was still in his bed, and he felt that he might never move again.

"I'm sorry," his mother said, and he could see the compassion on her face, and he realized that he had been needing to see it there.

His mother talked to him then, comforting him, but he heard only part of what she said. He heard her say that it appeared that Derry was not the girl they had thought her to be, that there were no two ways about it, Derry had treated him badly. He understood that while she had always liked Derry, she liked her less now. And Ron wondered if Derry deserved to be liked, the way she had treated him.

With the thought, the anger, he felt the tiniest wisp of energy run through his body. But he lacked the will even for anger.

And he felt that he shouldn't need his mother's sympathy as much as he did. He tried to tell his mother that he could handle it, but the words wouldn't come.

It wasn't that day but the next that his mother asked him if Derry had given him his presents back.

Ron, still lying on his bed, shook his head. He had given Derry only one present, the dresser set, and she still had it.

His mother widened her eyes. "I don't believe it," she said, meaning that she did. And then, "A girl is *supposed* to give a man his presents back when she stops going out with him."

Ron remembered having heard something of the kind. It wasn't a thing he would have thought of on his own, but he did remember hearing it. But the thought of the dresser set was almost more painful to him than the thought of Derry herself. He didn't want to think about it. "Let her keep it," he said. "I don't want it."

His mother sat down on a chair beside his bed and it was a moment before she spoke. "I understand how you feel," she said. "But Derry shouldn't be let get away with a thing like that. She ought to be shown."

Ron shook his head. "No," he said.

29

His mother gave her head a little shake, as if to say that Ron hadn't understood what she meant. "I don't want to tell you what to do," she said, "but Derry would respect you a lot more if you *didn't* let her get away with it. If you asked her for it back. It would be the manly thing to do."

Ron said nothing, but he was listening.

But when his mother spoke again it was as if she had changed her mind. "At your age nobody would think anything of it if you didn't do a thing," she said. "A man wouldn't put up with it, but nobody would think anything of it if you just walked away from the whole thing."

Ron saw then that asking for his present back was a thing he should do, that his mother would think less of him if he didn't do it. And it seemed to him that he would think less of himself.

"It isn't a thing anybody else can do for you," his mother said. "There are some things in this life that you've got to do for yourself."

That seemed to Ron very right and very true. You couldn't argue with it. And what was the tiny feeling of unwillingness that he had but a kind of cowardice? There were duties a man couldn't shirk no matter how much he might want to.

He walked to Derry's house not really thinking, just putting one foot in front of the other. But as he opened her front gate and started up the walk to her house, the Derry he pictured ahead of him at the door was the Derry he had always seen there, and he was in practice at loving Derry, not at showing her something. What if this was not the right thing to do? What if there was some flaw in his mother's thinking?

But he couldn't bear the thought of uncertainty. Start thinking this way and he would be back in bed again, unable to lift his head off the pillow. He had thought about it and made his decision and now he had come to the time to act upon it. He knocked at the door.

Derry's eyes widened when she heard what he had to say, and he saw both hurt and disbelief in them. But this turned quickly to contempt, a contempt that seemed to be endless, and he understood that his mother's belief that Derry would respect him for this was not true, and that it never could have been true. It seemed to him that this was something that he had to do something about.

But the thought did not stay with him. Derry came back with the dresser set and, in despair and a last-minute attempt to undo what he had done, Ron said, "Look, keep it. It's yours. I want you to have it."

But Derry's look of contempt only deepened. "I wouldn't touch it with a ten-foot pole," she said.

Then Ron was back on the street, with a shell-shaped box in his hand, and no place to go except home. He walked along remembering that he had something to do, but he couldn't remember what it was. He only knew that there was something still waiting to be done, and that whatever it was, it was still ahead of him, waiting for him to do it.

CÁLLING HOME

Her legs weren't straight any more, but bowed with arthritis, but she set her feet down with purpose. At the door of the church she paused for a moment, searching her purse for a piece of Kleenex. It wasn't that she expected to cry at Flora Neville's funeral, although she would have been happy enough to be overcome by tears, but that locating a Kleenex was a ritual she performed before entering upon any occasion. When she found it, Mrs. Robinson entered the church and accepted a printed folder—"a program," she called it—from one of the undertaker's men. Then she signed her name in the guest book, and it was the first name there.

Mrs. Robinson didn't ask the undertaker's man if Flora's coffin would be open. Coffins hardly ever were nowadays, and Mrs. Robinson didn't like asking questions to which the answer might be no. It gave her the feeling of being refused something.

Mrs. Robinson had made up her mind in advance about where she would sit: a seat on the aisle, about two-thirds of the way up to the front. It was not so far forward that you couldn't see some of the congregation, and not so far back that you couldn't catch glimpses of the family. "The mourners," Mrs. Robinson thought.

Mrs. Robinson attended all of the funerals that were held in Willow Bunch, even if she didn't know the people very well. "I hate to see a poor turnout at a funeral," she would say. "It's hard on the family when there isn't a good turnout."

She spoke as if going to funerals was a thing that she did out of neighbourliness, out of Christian charity, but the truth was, she thought, that there was a certain pleasure in being there. A funeral *meant* something, she thought. Ordinarily, life went along and what happened didn't matter very much one way or the other, but when somebody died, something had happened and you *knew* it. Things would never be quite the same again. It was a situation that provoked thought and invited reflection. It was also, quite often, an occasion for strong emotion, and Mrs. Robinson had a taste for strong emotion.

She didn't expect to get very much of it today.

Both Harley and Flora Neville were oldtimers, and both of them were active in the church, so there would be a big turnout. But there wouldn't be very many tears shed, or that was Mrs. Robinson's opinion.

But when Mrs. Robinson thought that, she rerouted her

33

thoughts, shuttled them to the back of her mind. There were thoughts that she considered it proper to have, and thoughts that she considered improper, and it seemed to her that it was improper to think too *exactly* of the dead, at least until they were decently underground.

And not only improper. Unwise. To think too exactly of Flora Neville right now might spoil something, prevent her from entering into the funeral in the proper spirit. Mrs. Robinson thought that going to a funeral was something like reading a book or watching a hockey game. You had to put something into it if you wanted to get something out of it.

For Allison Crawford, waiting next door in the rectory for the funeral to begin, the problem was not the same. Allison was Flora Neville's daughter, her first-born. She was sitting alone in the rectory living-room, looking out of the rectory window, and what she wanted was not to feel more, nor to feel less, but to feel clearly. She thought of the way that people sometimes asked about the bereaved. "How is he taking it?" they would ask. Or "How is she taking it?" And there were two answers to the question. You could say, "He's taking it pretty well." Or you could say, "He's taking it hard."

There was no question of taking it hard, of course, but beyond that, there were certain perplexities. Allison wanted to mourn her mother, she felt a need to mourn her. But she also felt as if a rule had been laid down for her. What the rule said was: *Mourn. But only as much as is honest.* But Allison wasn't sure what the rule meant, not exactly.

Allison had been wondering what it meant, how she was supposed to live with it, ever since she had heard about her mother's death. She had thought that when she had crossed the country, certain things would become clear to her, that when she was with her aunt, or her father, or her sister, she would suddenly *know* how she ought to feel. But it hadn't worked out that way.

Her father had met her at the highway confectionery that served as Willow Bunch's bus-stop. He had come out of the store as the bus was pulling in and had been standing at the foot of the bus steps as she got off.

"So you made it," he said.

"Yes," Allison said. "I made it."

Her "making it" had never been in any doubt, and Allison knew that her father did not mean to suggest that it had been. It was simply that this was what he always said when anyone arrived here from someplace else.

Allison and her father did not hug, did not kiss. The Nevilles had never been a hugging and a kissing family. Allison—back at the rectory, back at the window, back to *now*—thought that she had been hugged a good deal since she had come home, but not by her own family. Outsiders, people in whose families such things were done as a matter of course, had hugged and kissed her, but her own family had not. Instead they had met each other awkwardly, unsurely. It was as if they knew that hugging was called for, but they didn't know how to go about it, at least not with each other. Allison had wanted to hug her father, but she had not wanted, at a time like this, to seem to be forcing the ways of her own world upon him. Now she was sorry she hadn't done it.

Allison's father was wearing a windbreaker and slacks, his usual dress, but he had put on a tie, and Allison supposed that he felt the need of this formality to mark the death. When they got to the pickup, which her father had brought instead of the car, Allison saw that it was newly washed.

They got in, and, although her father had parked in the shade and left the windows open, the upholstery was hot. "Jessie's waiting for us down at the Co-op," her father said.

Jessie was Allison's aunt, her mother's sister. She had lived in Willow Bunch when Allison was growing up, but she lived in the city now.

"When did Jessie get down?" Allison asked.

"She came down with me..." Her father's voice trailed off. "When I came down from the hospital," he finished.

Her father backed the truck out from the confectionery and steered it onto the highway. "I asked Jessie to meet your bus with me," he said. "But she said she had some things she wanted to pick up." Her father's voice was determinedly normal. "I think she wanted to give us a chance to be alone," he said.

Allison smiled. Her father was not likely to say anything to her that he could not have said with the whole world listening, but it was like Jessie to want to give him the chance.

"She's staying on the farm then?"

Her father nodded. "It'll be the last time, I guess."

Allison felt a stir of sadness. Her parents had bought a house in town and had been about to move when her mother was taken ill. Now her father would be moving alone. Their house, the house that Allison had grown up in, would be left empty.

Allison felt the need to say something to her father, something that would take the place of the kiss she had not given him. But all she could think of was, "How are *you* making out, Dad?"

"Not too bad," her father said. It was what he always said. Only ordinarily he would have added, "Still livin', I guess," and today he just said, "Not too bad" a second time.

Driving in Willow Bunch didn't take much attention. Allison could feel her father reaching for something to say, something that would sum up what they were living through. Finally, "These things happen, I guess," he said.

Allison said nothing, and after a minute her father spoke again. "We were lucky it happened the way it did," he said.

Again Allison was silent. Her mother had had cancer, but she had died of a stroke, of a series of strokes, and Allison had been relieved that it had turned out that way. But she had also been guilty about her own relief. Her mother wouldn't have wanted it that way, she knew. Her mother would have wanted a chance to fight her cancer, to face it down, to outsmart it.

They left the highway and crossed the railway tracks into the town. "I'm glad you had the trip," Allison said finally.

"So am I," her father said. "We had a real good time. Practically the whole trip."

Just before her mother went into the hospital, her parents had gone on a bus tour to California. They had sent her postcards from Disneyland, from Knott's Berry Farm. "Having the time of our lives," they had written. Then they had come home and her mother's cancer had been diagnosed, and it was already inoperable.

Allison's father wrote to tell her. "They've decided to go straight into radiation," he wrote, "and they may give her some chemotherapy. Your mother's taking it wonderful. But it would be nice if you could manage to come home for a while."

Her father had not written "Come soon," but that was the message that Allison took from his letter. She put the letter down and went to the telephone to make airline reservations. Then she phoned home.

Her mother was excited, pleased at being phoned, pleased, seemingly, about everything. "They've decided to go straight into radiation with me," she said, and the way she spoke, you would have thought it was a matter of pride not to be treated like other patients. "At least *I* won't have to give all *my* bathing suits away," she said.

Main Street when they reached it was almost empty of cars, and Jessie was waiting in the shade in front of the Co-op for them. Allison opened the truck door for her aunt and for a moment the two women leaned, or almost leaned, toward each other, as if they might embrace, but neither of them made the decisive move. Then Allison slid across the truck

37

seat, closer to her father, to make room for Jessie.

They left the town, and the countryside looked as it should look, Allison thought. Summer was heavy on the land, and the hills in the distance were blue, and the grain in the fields was filling. Now and again the song of a meadowlark rose from a grassy knoll or fencepost.

"I always forget how pretty it is here," Allison said.

"It's not bad," her father said, dismissing it. "But you ought to see the redwoods."

He began then to talk about his trip, about the places he and her mother had visited, and Allison realized that this was his way of talking about her mother. "We saw about everything there *was* to see," he said. "The redwoods. The Mormon Temple. Disneyland."

"A different place every day, Flora said," Jessie contributed.

"We had two days in Las Vegas," her father said. "Two days and two nights." He adjusted the side vent of the window to produce more breeze. Then, to Allison, "Your mother kind of cut loose in Las Vegas," he said.

"*Mother* did?" Allison said. "*My mother?*" Her mother had been what was called "careful." "Your mother can pinch a penny till it cries," her father had used to say. For her mother, Allison thought, "cutting loose" in Las Vegas would mean buying a dollar's worth of nickels and losing them all in one casino.

"Those slot machines really got to her," her father said.

Allison waited, expecting a story, but it did not come, and when she glanced at her father, she saw that the skin on his cheekbones was tight. She did not ask him to go on.

"Flora said that trip was the best time she *ever* had," Jessie said, but Allison wondered why her aunt spoke with so much energy, as if she were refuting something.

"At least it took her mind off the cancer," her father said.

Allison was startled. "But Mother didn't know about the cancer *before* the trip," she wanted to say. "If she had known,

38

she wouldn't have gone. She would have stayed home and had it taken care of."

Aloud she said nothing.

They drove in silence for a while. Then, "How are Nanette and Wade?" she asked.

"Tip-top," her father said. "Couldn't be better."

Allison smiled. It was the sort of report she might have expected to get from her father. He always told you how things ought to be, not how things were. She would have to wait until she saw Nanette and Wade to see how things were with them really. Neither her sister nor her brother wrote often and even if they had, the things that matter in anyone's life are not the sort of things that get into letters.

They crossed the river and began to climb into the high land to the north of it. The leaves on the trees here were small, Allison noticed; there must have been drought early in the year. But the crops were looking good, she thought. But then she wondered if she knew how to judge these things any longer; she had been so long away.

One member of her family had hugged her, thought Allison, sitting at the rectory window, waiting for the funeral to begin. Nanette, coming over on Allison's first night home, had hugged her...but it had not been a natural hug, the kind that sisters or friends exchange. Instead it had been a *sloppy* hug, the kind that drunks give to each other. At first Allison had thought that Nanette *was* drunk, but then she saw that she was not. It was just that this was the way that Nanette had learned to hug people.

Allison had been aware of a desire to step back out of Nanette's embrace. There was something abject about the way that Nanette hugged, she had felt, something lacking in pride. But as soon as she had the thought, she rejected it. Where was the room here for pride? They were two sisters, mourning the death of their mother. If they couldn't hug

39

now, when could they hug?

Allison embraced Nanette firmly, trying not to be brisk about it. But then Nanette clung to her a little longer than she would have liked, and Allison could feel her heels tightening in an effort not to back away. She was also aware of Jessie in the room, and aware that she and Jessie had just been talking about Nanette, and that made it harder to be spontaneous.

"Where are Bill and Tara?" Allison asked finally.

"Out in the yard with Pop," Nanette said.

They stood there then, looking at each other, aware that the hug had not crossed the distance between them. Finally, "This isn't the happiest of times," Nanette said.

"No."

"Still, we were lucky it happened the way it did," Nanette said.

Allison stiffened. There it was again. *Luck.* Why did people always want to mention luck when someone died? When someone died after a long illness, people said that it was a blessing, and Allison could see that. But when someone died after no illness at all, one day dancing the schottische, the next day stiff and cold in a box, people found reason to rejoice then too. "It's the way to go," they would say. "The way I'd want to go myself."

Even in the most unlikely deaths, people found blessings to count. Once a friend of Allison's, a young mother with young children, had been killed in a car accident. Here, you would have thought, there could be no consolation. But after the funeral, "We were so lucky," the friend's sister told Allison. "The children could have been with her. They could all have been killed."

It was as if human beings had some born-in need to feel grateful, Allison thought. As if they had to believe that there was somebody up there, making sure that things happened as they should.

But it wasn't *only* that, Allison knew. She had heard these same things from people who believed, as she did herself, that if there was anybody up there, it was somebody with no concern at all for human beings.

Allison felt no inclination to prove to herself that she was lucky. There might be nothing you could do about death, she thought, but you didn't have to give it your approval.

"She could have had months of suffering," Nanette said.

"I suppose she could have."

"It was easier on her and easier on Pop," Nanette said. "That it happened this way."

"If it had to happen at all," Allison said.

Nanette had come over early to help Allison get ready for the callers who would come, and they set to work filling the coffee urn, setting cups on saucers, slicing carrot loaf and banana bread that neighbours had brought over. Their father came in with Bill and Tara, Nanette's nine-year-old, but he excused himself almost at once. "I hope you folks won't mind if I disappear tonight," he said. "I've got kind of a headache. I'm afraid I wouldn't be very good company for anybody."

He wanted to be alone, Allison realized, but he didn't want to say so.

"You go ahead, Dad," she said. "We'll see to things down here."

"It's not much of a thing to do," her father said. "Go upstairs when you're expecting company."

"They'll understand," Allison said. But she herself felt surprised. If her father was going upstairs when he would have been expected to stay down, it was because there was an intensity of feeling there that she had not expected.

Her father went upstairs and the rest of them went into the living-room to wait. "Why don't you buy us a drink, Bill?" Nanette asked. "I know Pop's got some liquor stashed away in

41

the kitchen someplace."

Allison was smiling. It was a long time since she had heard the expression: *buy us a drink* she thought.

Bill spoke. "If you want to tie one on, that's your business, Nanette," he said. "But it seems to me that there are better times than this to do it."

There was a coldness in Bill's voice that shocked Allison. It was not the way that anyone ought to speak to a woman who had just lost her mother, she thought. Especially was it not the way a husband ought to speak to his wife. Was this the way that things were with Nanette now? she wondered.

Allison had known before she came home that Nanette drank too much. But she wasn't sure, in Nanette's case, exactly what "too much" meant. Did Nanette drink and wake up the next morning with a headache? Did she drink and get amorous—mushy—at parties? Was she a sloppy drunk, leaning on people, demanding some impossible degree of oneness with the rest of the world? Did she lose her balance, pass out, throw up on her friends' broadloom? Or was she a quiet and secret drinker, never quite sober, never quite able to call on her own intelligence, but no embarrassment to her family either? Allison didn't know.

"I could make us some tea," she said. "We could go into the kitchen and make it together."

"Tea wasn't exactly what I had in mind," Nanette said sardonically.

"Try some banana bread, then," Allison said.

Tea wasn't what Allison had in mind either. What Allison had in mind was talk. Talk with her sister. She wanted to know how things were with Nanette, but she wanted to know how things had been with her mother too. She wanted to know what her mother had been like at the last, first facing cancer, and then attacked by the strokes. But even as she recognized what she wanted, Allison knew that this was the wrong time to think about it. Callers were expected. They would have to be dealt with first.

Condolence calls: is there any right way to make them? Allison, who had often been a caller, tried, now that she was the called-upon, to make it easy for people, to help the conversation along. She sensed that people didn't know exactly what to say about her mother, or whether to mention her at all, and she wanted to make it clear to them that they could talk about anything, her mother included. *It shouldn't be so hard*, she thought with a flash of resentment. *There must be something that can be said about her.*

But people avoided the subject. One man wanted to talk about Allison and Nanette, what they had been like as children. "What a pair you were!", he said. "Always into something!"

And Allison smiled as if she, too, remembered. The truth was, she thought, that she and Nanette had not always been into something. *Nanette* had been a spunky child, capable of getting into things, but Allison had not. She had been well behaved, too well behaved.

But perhaps the man had spoken of their childhood only as a means of getting into his own. He was talking now of the "devilment" he and his brother had got into, of what "the old man" had said and done when he had caught them.

They were standard stories of childhood: no truth to them. Listening, Allison felt a kind of wonder. Out of old scoldings and old spankings and old displays of temper, stories are made. And all of the stories say the same thing: kids are like that; parents do what they have to do. It was as if everyone had the same childhood, Allison thought. There was no injustice in these stories, and there were no cases of insufficient love. You would have thought that there were no imperfect parents, and no unacceptable childhoods. But why did the stories come out on an occasion like this? Because,

Allison realized, there was a prohibition in this room and it affected everybody. What the prohibition said was: *let us not be honest.*

When talk finally did turn to Allison's mother, what people said was what a wonderful gardener she had been, how there was nobody who could beat Flora when it came to sweet peas, how they would never forget the zinnias she put in the flower show two years ago. It was her mother and yet not her mother they were talking about, Allison thought.

She was grateful to the callers, who meant it as a gift, but it was a relief when they went home.

"Okay, *now* I'll scare us up a drink," Nanette said, coming back from the door. "I know where Pop keeps his hooch."

Allison and Tara spoke at the same time. What Allison said was: "I could use a drink." What Tara said was: "I want to go home."

"You hear that, Nanette?" Bill said. "Tara's tired. She wants to go home."

"Oh, honey," Nanette said, speaking to Tara. "I haven't had a chance to talk to your Auntie Allison yet. You find yourself a blanket and curl up for a few minutes. Come on, Allison. I'll help you clean up the kitchen."

Bill put on his Massey-Ferguson cap and shoved it to the back of his head. Half-way between going and staying, Allison thought. Tara found her blanket and Jessie went upstairs.

In the kitchen, Nanette opened the door of the cupboard in which their father kept his liquor. "What's yours?" she asked.

"Scotch, I guess."

Nanette poured two drinks, not bothering with a jigger. "First one today," she said, raising her glass.

When Nanette poured a second drink she did not say, "First one today." She said, "The blood of Jesus," and Allison was shocked, not by her words but by the way she said them. There was a cadence to them, as if they were words that Nanette said often.

44

Nanette had changed a good deal since Allison's last trip home. She was only mildly overweight, but she had a puffy-in-her-clothes appearance that made her look fatter than she was. She was no longer pretty. And Nanette, who had always been so slangy, so tough-talking, still had a coating of her old breeziness, but it was accompanied, often, by a note of apology. And also of resentment. It was as if Nanette was saying, "I'm not much," and then turning on you as if you had said it. And she had developed a way of lifting her voice at the end of her sentences, as if to ask your approval. Their mother had not been like that, Allison thought. She did a thing and you could like it or lump it.

"Nanette," Allison said, "did Mother know she had cancer before she went on that trip?"

The callers had washed the teacups and the cake plates before they left, but the counter was covered with pans of cake and loaves of fruit bread. Nanette was re-wrapping a loaf that had been cut into during the evening.

She turned away from the counter. "She found the lump before she left," Nanette said. "And she went to see the doctor."

"But didn't the doctor tell her to have it seen to right away?" Allison asked.

Nanette gave a lopsided smile. "Well, *after* the trip, when it turned out that it was cancer and it was too late to operate, Mother said that the doctor told her that there was nothing to worry about."

"But that isn't what she said before?"

"That isn't what she said before."

Allison understood. Their mother couldn't bear to know what she had done to herself. "But even so..." she said.

"You mean why would she take the chance? Why did she go on the trip?"

Allison nodded.

"Why did Mother do anything?" Nanette said. She had

45

found a plastic box and was stacking the foil-wrapped loaves inside it. "Maybe she just wanted to see Disneyland," she said.

Allison felt wonder, as she often had before, at the strength of her mother's will, at her determination not to be thwarted. "I suppose she didn't tell anyone," she said.

Nanette hesitated for a minute. "Well, she didn't tell Pop. And she didn't tell me," she said.

"Who did she tell?" Allison asked quietly.

Nanette shrugged. "She told Wade," she said. "Which is just about the same thing as keeping it to yourself."

"Wade!" Allison said. "But didn't Wade tell her to stay home and have it taken care of?"

Nanette shook her head wearily. "I don't know what Wade told her," she said.

Allison felt bewildered. *Wade,* she thought. *Wade.* Wade was her brother, but it sometimes seemed to her that he was a person she hardly knew. Wade was much younger than she and Nanette, and when they were children she had given no thought to knowing him. It hadn't occurred to her that there might be anything there to know. But since they had grown up, when Allison came home on visits, it seemed to her that she could never really connect with Wade in conversation.

Nanette sat down again with her drink in front of her. "Can you stay for a while after the funeral, Allison?" she asked. "Somehow we've got to get Pop packed up and moved to town."

Allison looked around her mother's kitchen, trying to imagine the familiar utensils and knick-knacks packed into boxes, to reappear in some other house. One of the things she had not been prepared for, she thought, was the power of *things* to move her: for the sight of recipes Scotch-taped to the inside of cupboard doors, for the slant of sunlight coming through windows so clean that they might have been washed for a competition. And to have to handle all of the things that her mother had accumulated over the years, to have to decide what to keep and what to give away....

"I can stay as long as I'm needed," she told Nanette.

"I'm glad," Nanette said.

Allison's glass was empty, and so was Nanette's. "I feel like a cup of tea," Allison said. "How about you?"

Nanette smiled ruefully. "I'd just as soon have another scotch," she said.

Bill's voice came from the doorway, startling them. "Haven't you had enough?" he demanded.

Nanette was instantly hostile. "God, can't I do anything without having you breathing down my neck?" she said.

"Look, if you want to make a night of it, you go right ahead," Bill said. "Only remember, this time it's *your* mother's funeral."

Allison watched a change come over Nanette. "Bill, that wasn't my fault," Nanette said.

But Bill was speaking to Allison. "Your little sister here just about slid into the grave when we buried my mother," he said. "We had to haul her out by the elbows."

"The ground was wet," Nanette said.

"Nobody else fell in, that's all I can say," Bill said.

Allison found speech. "Okay, Bill. That's enough," she said.

Bill laughed, without humour. "You don't have to worry about Nanette, Allison," Bill said. "She's feeling no pain. This isn't the first time she's been out to the kitchen tonight, you know."

But Bill was being unfair, Allison knew. Her sister was drinking, but she was not drunk. She had not been sneaking drinks all evening. She could not have been. Not this evening, anyway.

The next morning Allison's father went out, leaving the place to Allison and Jessie. Allison looked for something to do.

There was a large bouquet of flowers sitting on top of the television set in the living-room. Someone had typed the names of the people who had gone together to buy it on to a wide white satin ribbon, which was attached to a leaf with a paper clip. Allison removed it. But then she put it back again. People would be expecting to see it there, she thought.

There was nothing to do. There was only time to put in. Allison made a pot of tea and sat down at the kitchen table with Jessie. "Maybe you'd better tell me about Nanette's drinking," she said.

"What about it?" Jessie said.

"Does she have it under control?"

"I suppose it depends on what you mean by 'under control,'" Jessie said.

"I mean is she an alcoholic?" Allison said bluntly.

Jessie shook her head, as if to say that she was no good at definitions. "I wouldn't know about that," she said. "But Nanette does hit the bottle pretty hard sometimes."

The day passed. The night before, Wade had been expected, but Wade had not come. And that night, when all of them were to go to the funeral home together, Wade did not come either.

"Don't worry about Wade," her father said. "He'll be at the church tomorrow."

But Allison could see that her father was hurt, and she was angry. She could understand Wade not *wanting* to come to the funeral home. She was a modern young woman and she did not believe that there was any point in looking at the dead either. You ought to try to remember them as they had been in life, she thought. But her father had wanted his children there—together as a family for one last time, she imagined him thinking—and Wade should have put his personal feelings aside.

48

It was anger with Wade that Allison was feeling as they entered the funeral home and walked across the grey carpet to the grey box in which her mother lay. But there, in the presence of death, anger left her, and a kind of wonder took its place. It seemed to her that something profound was happening to her. Generation upon generation of mankind had looked upon their dead, she thought. Now she was one of them.

She stood looking at the woman who had been her mother, and what she felt was distance. Such a short time dead, she thought, and already so far away. She imagined a tunnel, and her mother receding down it, leaving behind the figure that lay here. *So* dead, she thought. Clay returned to clay. But then it seemed to her that she had seen clay pots that were more alive than this figure, more capable of speech. She had no feeling that this body might speak, that it had ever spoken.

She had been expecting something else, she realized. But what was it? *Outrage,* she thought. That was what she had been expecting her mother's face to show. Nanette had told her that that was what her mother had felt after her stroke. She had wanted to do battle with her cancer, and the stroke was cheating her of that chance.

But this face did not show outrage, nor sorrow, nor pain. It did not show anything. Allison would scarcely have known that it was her mother.

But then she saw something, something in the set of the jaw, that *was* her mother. It was as if her mother's jaw was sending her a message. It was an expression that Allison had seen on her mother's face before, and often. But now, on a dead face, she could put no name to what the expression was.

When they returned to the farm Wade and Brenda were there, waiting for them. Wade was sitting straddled on a kitchen chair, an Allis-Chalmers cap on the back of his head.

He did not get up as they came in. "Well, Sis," he said to Allison. "How are things with you?"

Allison's anger returned. *My mother has just died,* she felt like saying. *How are things with you?*

"Okay, I guess," she said.

Wade nodded. "Tough luck, eh?" he said.

"Yes," Allison said. "Very tough."

It was not Wade's choice of words that offended Allison. She had grown up surrounded by men who had no words for dealing with things like death. She remembered a neighbour who had been able to say only "Son of a gun" when his wife had died. He had said it over and over again. What offended Allison was the feeling that for Wade, "Tough luck" really covered the situation.

She plugged in the kettle to make tea for all of them, but her father excused himself and so did Jessie. She was left alone with Wade and Brenda.

They tried to talk, or Allison did. Wade kept his responses brief, forcing Allison to come out further and further if she wanted to keep the conversation going at all. *You come to me*: that was what Wade was saying.

At last Allison lost patience with talk that said nothing, with a brother who controlled by withdrawal. "I understand that Mother told you about her lump before she went on the trip," she said. It had to be talked about, she thought. You couldn't not know a thing like that.

"She mentioned it," Wade said.

"And what did you tell her?"

"I told her what she wanted to hear," Wade said. "I told her to take the trip."

"For Christ's sake, Wade! *Cancer.*"

"Well, how was I to know?"

"You didn't have to take the chance."

"*I* didn't take the chance," Wade said. "Mother did. She made her own decision."

50

You discover that your brother is a killer and what do you do? Allison thought. *She* wanted time to think about it, to put it in some perspective. It might be that if you looked at it in a different way, it would appear differently to you. She could feel that she was about to retreat from honesty.

"It might have been too late even before she went on the trip," she said finally.

"That's what *I* think," Wade said.

"Wade or no Wade," Allison said, "it's Mother I can't understand."

It was the next morning, the morning of the funeral, and Allison and Jessie were alone in the house again. "Mother wasn't stupid," Allison went on. "She knew about cancer. She knew what the rules were."

"Your mother never thought any of the rules applied to her," Jessie said.

That was true, Allison thought; that had to be acknowledged. It might not have mattered *what* Wade told her; if her mother had made up her mind to take the trip, she would have taken it. Her mother would have thought that if she just had enough nerve, if she didn't lose her nerve, she would be able to outsmart her cancer, and then it would be behind her.

"It's not that I'm trying to pretend that she was like everyone else," Allison said.

Jessie smiled ruefully. "How could you?" she asked.

From where they were sitting at the kitchen table, Allison could see a china ornament on a corner shelf, a southern belle with hooped skirts and a parasol, a sentimental thing, too appealing to Allison's eyes. But she knew that she had not always seen it that way. When she first saw it, she had thought it beautiful.

It was while Allison was still in high school, and she and her mother had been shopping together, not in Willow

Bunch but in a bigger town nearby. They were in Macleod's Hardware when Allison had spotted the figurine and drawn it to her mother's attention. They had stood there side by side, admiring it together. And then her mother had stolen it.

Allison could not remember when she first knew that her mother was a thief. It seemed to her that she had always known it. But this was the first time that her mother had ever taken anything right in front of her eyes. She had come into the store with her mother, had agreed to go shopping with her, *because* she thought that her mother wouldn't take anything while she was being watched. She had thought that if she stayed at her mother's elbow every minute, everything would be all right. Now she knew better.

Allison marched out the door, leaving her mother in the store, and climbed into the truck. Shame was a feeling she had grown up with, but lately she had learned to turn it into rage, and that was less painful. "I'll tell her exactly what I think of her," Allison thought. "I'll really tell her."

But when her mother came out to the truck it was all Allison could do to speak. She felt as if her throat was paralyzed. "I'll never go into a store with you again," she said finally.

Her mother made her eyes wide. "Allison, I don't know what you mean," she said.

Allison knew that her voice was going to squeak, and it did. "I mean what you've got in your shopping bag," she said.

"The ornament?" her mother said calmly. "Allison, that ornament was priced away too high." She spoke as if that justified it, as if Macleod's was just asking for it. As if *she* were the injured party, Allison thought.

Allison, the grown-up Allison, often thought that she would never have made it through the years of her childhood if it had not been for Jessie, for her sane presence. She turned to Jessie when these things happened, and Jessie let her.

"I told her she ought to be ashamed of herself," Allison said.

"And do you know what she said then? She said: 'Your father and I have spent a lot of money in that store over the years.'"

Jessie smiled. "Your mother's logic," she said.

"But how can she be that way?" Allison demanded.

"I don't know," Jessie said wearily. "Just be glad you're not that way."

That was one of Jessie's sayings: *Be glad you're not that way.* Another was: *We're judged by what we are, not who we're related to.* And another was: *Remember, people see her good points as well as her bad.* Allison didn't really believe any of them, but it helped her to hear them just the same. When she talked to Jessie, she could sometimes move outside of the situation, find a place where she could look down on it from a distance. She could almost believe then that it wouldn't go on forever.

The shame of being their mother's daughters: once it had been the foremost fact of Allison's and Nanette's lives. Wade had been younger; he hadn't known what was going on, Allison thought. But for herself and Nanette, life had been a constant dread of exposure, a constant basting in shame.

Their shame, and their instinct for hiding it, had been so great that they didn't even speak to each other about their mother's stealing. It was not until Allison's last year at home that one of them spoke of it to the other. But once they had begun, Allison thought, they never spoke of anything else. They brought forth their separate humiliations one by one and spread them before each other like gifts.

"You know how Mum used to phone her grocery orders in to the Red and White and then have Pop pick them up?" Nanette said one day. "Only then she would always phone back and tell Lavina that something was missing. A pound of butter or a can of Prem or something. She would say it was on the bill, but not in the grocery box.

"Well, I don't think I ever thought very much about it. If I had, I suppose it would have seemed funny to me that the Red and White could make so many mistakes. Or maybe I did think that. But she always seemed to get away with it, so I suppose I thought that nobody noticed. That the Red and White would get so many orders that it wouldn't be able to keep track of a thing like that.

"Anyway, I was in the Red and White on my lunch hour from school one day when the phone rang and Lavina answered it. And as soon as I heard her say 'Hello, Flora' I had the feeling that something funny was going to happen."

"I don't know if I want to hear this," Allison said, but she did. Under her dread of knowing there was a kind of greed to know. It was as if somebody had assigned her to find out all there was to know about her mother, to make sure that nothing would surprise her.

"Anway, Mum said something to Lavina, and then Lavina said, 'I'm sorry to have to contradict you, Flora, but those raisins were *so* in there.' And then Mum said something else and Lavina spoke back, as smooth as silk. 'We've developed a special way of handling your orders, Flora,' she said. 'I get the things together, and then Stanley checks them off the list as I put them into the box. That way there's two of us know that nothing is missing.'"

This had happened two years before and Nanette was only now telling Allison. "What did you do then?" Allison asked.

"What do you think I did?" Nanette said. "I just about died."

How had they lived with it: the shame, the fear of exposure? The grownup Allison had no answer to that question. The fear of exposure, at least, shouldn't have bothered them the way it did, she thought. If a person went in for stealing or even just for "cutting corners"—for chiselling—in a town the size of Willow Bunch, everybody was going to know about it. And her mother, as it happened, went in for both. "If there's a way to pull a fast one, Flora Neville will pull it," people had said.

The chiselling had bothered Allison even more than the

stealing. She had dreaded any social occasion. When there was a party at the school or the Legion Hall, all the ladies brought lunch and Allison's mother did too. But her mother always put her cake or pan of squares on a bottom shelf in the hall kitchen, hoping that it wouldn't be found so she could take it home again.

But people were on to her. "Where has she put it this time?" they would say. It was a sort of joke, a game with them. "We can't let her get away with that," they would say.

Then as now, teas were held after funerals, and friends brought baking to help out. Her mother would bring a cake like everyone else, but her mother would leave her cake in the car. "It's there in case you run short," she would tell the ladies in the kitchen. "But if you don't need it, I'd just as soon take it around to the house for the family."

Only she never did take it around to the house, and people checked up to find out that she hadn't. It gave people a sort of grim satisfaction to catch her mother in the act, Allison thought. They were on to her. They let her get away with nothing.

"Why doesn't she get wise to herself?" Nanette had demanded once. "Does she think that people don't notice? Does she think that people don't talk?"

Allison had nodded miserably. Her mother did think that, she suspected, or something very like it. Probably the question of whether or not people would talk was never permitted to be posed in her mind. When she was caught in the act, as it were, she would be stiff with the people who had caught her —eventually she was stiff with nearly everyone—but she didn't seem to think that what had happened would continue in any way into the future. It was as if she did not believe that people had memories. As if she thought that you could always go back to the beginning again, to the clean slate.

By the time Allison had finished high school, there wasn't a store in town that her mother could go into. One by one, the storekeepers had caught her stealing and told her not to come in anymore.

"She'll come in and pick out her groceries and pay for them," the Co-op manager told Allison's father. "Then she'll go back into the store and walk around putting things into her bag. Today we caught her with a tin of sandwich spread and a Sweet Marie chocolate bar. I'm sorry as hell, Harley."

Allison imagined her father receiving this news. He would look as if he wasn't hearing anything, she thought. Or as if he weren't there at all.

"Your father is as honest as the day is long," Jessie had said. "Everyone knows that." It was another one of her aunt's sayings, but this one was true, Allison thought.

Allison's father had never had it out with his wife about her stealing. He had never been able to think of the one perfect action to take and so he had done nothing. He had pretended that it hadn't happened and when he couldn't do that, he pretended that it wouldn't happen again.

Once Allison had demanded that her father "do something," and he had pretended at first that he didn't know what she was talking about. But when she insisted, "What good would it do?" he demanded. "Everybody would get all upset and what good would it do? It might even make things worse."

After that, Allison had given up on her parents, and concentrated all her energey on getting away from Willow Bunch. Her father would never speak up, she decided, and her mother would never change.

Nanette, however, did not want to get away. At seventeen she was already involved with Bill; she wanted to marry him and live her life in Willow Bunch. "All it takes is a certain maturity," she had said.

Fine, brave words! Allison thought of Nanette as she had been at seventeen, and Nanette as she was today, and a feeling of heavy sadness came over her. The subject of Nanette's drinking had come up last night when Allison was alone for a minute with Brenda, Wade's wife. "I suppose Mother being the way she was might have something to do with it," Allison had said.

"I don't know," Brenda said. "You don't drink. And Wade doesn't drink."

"How *has* Wade coped with it?" Allison asked. "Living right here all these years?"

"Wade?" Brenda said. "Wade doesn't have to cope. Wade doesn't feel anything about anything."

Now, sitting in her mother's kitchen, musing over her living and her dead, Allison found herself unwilling to be too hard on any of them. It was easy for me, she thought. When you live at the far end of the country, you don't have to face things. You can keep your distance; you can even be a dutiful daughter. *Pretty soft,* she imagined Nanette and Wade thinking.

And maybe it was. But she wasn't sorry. Moving away had meant that she had *had* a life, that she was able to keep a certain perspective on things. She told herself that, but the thought brought her a feeling of hollowness. *Is perspective enough?* she asked herself. *Isn't there something more that is needed?*

Yes, she thought; something was. What was wanted now was grief. And not the easy grief that the callers two nights ago had offered her. They had *translated* her mother for her, turning the woman who had really been her mother into someone else, a nicer woman, a woman they thought she would find easier to mourn. And she had been almost tempted to accept their version. It would have been nice to forget what her mother had been like, to pretend that she was another person, to be able to mourn her wholeheartedly. But Allison hadn't done it. She had felt something like loyalty to the woman who really had been her mother, to her right to be remembered as she really was. She had nodded and smiled while people spoke, but she had persisted in her own way of remembering. She had kept the picture whole. Because how could you grieve for an unreal person?

Sitting alone in the rectory on the day of the funeral, sitting by the window, Allison studied the street outside. She saw the people arriving for her mother's funeral, coming early because the church was small, and then lingering on the sidewalk outside. She saw the pallbearers, standing in a group, their heads bent earnestly, listening to the instructions of the undertaker's man. She saw the chairs stacked by the door of the church, ready to be set up on the lawn when the church was full.

People were gathered in little groups, exchanging greetings, and Allison could imagine the conversations. "How are things out your way?" "Pretty dry. That shower Tuesday missed us." The voices would be low but matter-of-fact; people wouldn't want to seem to be claiming more sorrow than they felt.

The undertaker's man stopped talking and the pallbearers shifted positions. One of them, Allison saw, had a red poppy in his lapel. He hadn't worn his suit since last November, she thought, and he hadn't looked in a mirror today. But as she was watching, the undertaker's man said something and all of the pallbearers smiled, and the man removed the poppy from his lapel and stuffed it into his pocket. "That'll save you a quarter next November," Allison imagined someone saying.

Allison had come to town early. Someone had been needed to pick up a bouquet of flowers that had come down from the city on the bus and Allison had volunteered. It would have been possible to get someone else to do it but Allison had thought that it would be good to be alone for a while. It was only as she was carrying the flowers into the church that she realized that she had another reason for coming, that there was a thing she wanted to do. She wanted to see her mother again.

Allison was surprised that this should be so, but she didn't question it. She asked one of the undertaker's men to open the coffin, and then she was standing in front of it, and looking down.

It was there all right, she thought. The look that she thought she had seen on her mother's face the night before. After she had left her mother she had doubted if she had seen anything, but it was there, all right. It was in the set of the jaw, and it seemed to Allison to be sending out a message. "*I* have nothing to be ashamed of," her mother's jaw was saying.

A blue car was approaching down the street. Watching from the rectory window, Allison thought at first that it was Nanette's and Bill's, but when it came closer she could see that someone else was driving, and that it was a different make of car than theirs. Once she had known every car in the country, Allison thought; now she didn't even know her own sister's.

Wade and Brenda came first. There was a space behind the hearse for family cars and Allison watched them pulling into it. When they were in the rectory with her, Allison spoke to Wade in an undertone. "Have you see Nanette today?" she asked.

Wade shook his head, but barely.

"I hope she's all right," Allison said.

Wade shrugged. "That's her lookout, isn't it?" he said.

When Nanette and Bill did get there, Allison was relieved to see that Nanette *was* all right. She was puffy-faced and unsteady, but it was not the unsteadiness of intoxication, but, possibly, of grief.

Any why not? Allison asked herself. Why not grief? We can't all three of us be deficient in feeling.

Her father was driving his own car. Allison watched him

pull in behind the hearse and he and Jessie got out. Then they came in and they all sat waiting together, and Allison saw her father looking at each of them in turn, fixing his eyes on them. It was as if he were taking a picture of them, she thought. Or as if he were embracing them.

Then it was time to go to the church. They checked their faces in mirrors and made last-minute visits to the toilet, and then they all went over together. Walking toward the church, Allison could hear the music of the organ reaching out to them. *Abide With Me.* Soon they would be singing the old, old hymns and listening to the old, old words. Hearing the music, Allison felt the tug of tears, but she resisted it. She did not want to weep because of words and music.

It was over, Allison thought. It was over and they had lived through it. Which proved that you could live through anything.

It was three days after the funeral and Allison felt the need to remind herself of this, because now the difficult time had come. She was sorting through her mother's things, packing up for her father's move to town. She was doing what women had always done in times of death, she thought. She was helping out. She was tidying up. She was doing what had to be done.

As she worked it seemed to Allison that there should be some ritual for this job, some ceremony for the handling of possessions, some gathering of daughters and grand-daughters which, because it followed prescribed forms, would make the job less painful.

She was thinking this when the telephone rang. It was the drugstore. "I'm glad I got *you,* Allison," the clerk said. "The thing is, we've got some pictures here that your mother sent away to be developed. I didn't know what to do with them."

"I'll come in and pick them up," Allison said.

She took her father's pickup and drove into town, and

when she got home again, she took the pictures out of their envelope. They were from the trip to California, she saw. Here was her father standing in front of a redwood tree; here was her mother shaking hands with Mickey Mouse. *What am I going to do with these things?* Allison thought.

But when her father came in and she told him about the pictures, it turned out that he saw these pictures as he would have seen any others: as something to look at, to take pleasure in. It was almost as if her mother was sitting beside him, looking at them too.

He went through them one by one. "This is our motel in Helena, Montana," he said. "This is your mother with the tour director."

They came to a picture of a palomino horse. "This is your mother with Trigger, Roy Rogers' old horse," he said. "They've got him stuffed and standing outside their place in the Mojave Desert."

And then they came to a picture in which a Hollywood fantasy of a building stood behind a score or more of jetting fountains. Allison's mother was a tiny figure in a turquoise pant-suit in the foreground. "This is Caesar's Palace in Las Vegas," he father said. "Prettiest place you ever saw in your life."

Allison didn't want to comment. "Is this where Mother lost all her money?" she asked instead. She had never heard the end of that story, she realized.

But when her father spoke, his voice shook. "No," he said. "That was at the Golden Nugget."

Allison looked at him for a minute. Then, "How much *did* she lose?" she asked quietly.

"We were each of us carrying $1000 worth of travellers' cheques," her father said. "She went through hers. And then she wanted to start in on mine."

"*A thousand dollars!*" Allison said.

"I know, it's hard to believe," her father said.

"I *can't* believe it," Allison said.

"Neither could I," her father said. "I just couldn't understand it. At the time."

Allison waited and the pain on her father's face deepened. "I think your mother got it into her head that if she could beat those slot machines, then she could beat the cancer too," he said.

It had the ring of truth. "But that's crazy," Allison said.

"Maybe it was and maybe it wasn't," her father said. "But I wish I'd given her the chance to try."

When her father left the house, Allison was near tears. She did not want to work, did not want to handle her mother's things right then, but she was afraid to stop. If she stopped, she thought, she might not be able to start again. So she worked on.

When she came to the drawer in which her mother kept her tea-towels, it occurred to her that the towels could be used as packing for glassware, so she opened the cupboard in which her mother kept her vases. There was a paper Scotch-taped to the inside of the door. It was an Altar Guild schedule and it covered the months just past and the months just ahead. 27 Sept. —*Decorate church for Harvest Festival,* Allison read. 29 Sept. —*Dismantling and disbursement of vegetables.*

Someone else would have to do these things now.

Allison remembered all the years that her mother had helped to decorate the church, taking flowers in summer and arrangements of dried grain or pine cones in winter. It had been a matter of pride with her mother that nobody had brought nicer flowers, or bigger ones, and that nobody else had done it for so long.

"Mum. Oh, Mum," Allison thought.

She brought her hands up and turned them into fists and pressed her knuckles into her cheeks to keep from crying. But she wept anyway. "Mum. Oh, Mum," she said.

The days passed and her father got moved, and it was time for Allison to return to her own home, but she wanted to visit her mother's grave before she left. It was not a thing that Allison thought that she should have wanted to do, but she was finding in herself a need to do all the old things that people had always done and she had decided to accept it.

She borrowed her father's truck and went to the cemetery alone. That was a thing that she wanted too.

She left the pickup on the road and walked in from the gate, passing row after row of stones marked with known names. She thought of city graveyards, where even your own needed a map to find you, where none you knew would ever pass by. This was better, she thought. You might be dead, but you would be, for a time, remembered.

The undertaker's artificial grass was gone from her mother's grave and the freshly-turned clay was not as moist as it had been. The flowers on the grave were beginning to wilt, but not as much as you would have expected, Allison thought.

She stood for a moment, waiting for the words that would tell her what she felt. Then she realized that there were no words. She bent over and began to pluck dead flowers out of the sprays. Still tidying up, she thought. And then, because her hands were full of dead flowers and she couldn't carry any more, she straightened up and began to walk toward the gate. She still had other farewells to say.

CITY WEDDING

When Astrid was married, the neighbours got together and held a shower for her at the schoolhouse. It was the first shower to be held in the district and Astrid had been proud and almost afraid that there would be people whose noses would be out of joint at seeing her so lucky. At the end of the evening, she had found an applebox in the school kitchen and packed all her presents in it, rejoicing in the can-opener, the crocheted pot-holders, the hot-dish mats. Astrid had never supposed that Billy's wedding would be like *that*, that all of Roxanne's shower presents would fit into one applebox. Just the same she had been disturbed when Billy had borrowed a truck to transport Roxanne's presents home. Astrid, in the city for the shower, watched silently as Billy carried Corningware casseroles and kitchen clocks and no-iron tablecloths out to the truck.

"It seems to me that things are getting a little bit out of hand," she said to herself. And then, "It makes you wonder."

Astrid would have liked to have told someone else that it seemed to her that things were getting a little bit out of hand, and that it made you wonder. She was staying at Sophie's house, where she always stayed when she came to the city, and Sophie was her sister, so she could have told Sophie.

She didn't, however. It seemed to her that if she said these things, even to Sophie, the spoken words would hang in her memory, making it difficult for her to do what she had made up her mind to do, which was to go along with things.

"It's the Bradys' affair, really," she told Sophie. "Whatever they decide on will be just fine with me."

She told Sheila Brady, Roxanne's mother, the same thing. "You don't have to ask me about everything," she said. "You know more about these things than I do."

It seemed to Astrid that she meant these things. She felt that she could trust Sheila to do the right thing before she could trust herself. But she also spoke out of a desire to let Sheila know that she, Astrid, wasn't fussy, wasn't *too particular*. Astrid took it for granted that it was not a good thing to be fussy or too particular.

Sheila, however, had greeted Astrid's words with a frown, almost as if she wanted Astrid to be hard to please. "The groom's mother is *supposed* to be consulted," Sheila said. She indicated the stack of wedding books and magazines that she had bought to help her plan the wedding, as if citing an authority. "We're supposed to give you a chance to tell us what you think," she said.

What Astrid thought was that it was all too much for her. There were to be five bridesmaids in crystalline, rented flowers for the wedding cars, orchid corsages for the mothers. She knew nothing about affairs like this. Just the same, and whatever she might say, she did like to be asked. She enjoyed the stately exchange of good manners: Sheila's good manners in consulting her, her own good manners in assuring Sheila that all of the arrangements being made were agreeable.

They were sitting in Sheila's living-room, and, Astrid thought, a stranger coming into the room could have told at once whose home it was. There was something about Sheila that seemed to go with the turquoise brocade of the sofa, with the ornamental gold plates around the light switches. Sheila was small and pretty, in a dark, blue-eyed, Irish way. She curved in and she curved out, and she had a way of moving that made you aware of these things. Astrid, who had none of these attributes, felt large and silent and Swedish beside her. Sheila was quick-moving, quick-speaking, quick-thinking. She could change her ground in the twinkling of an eye. Beside her, Astrid felt slow, confused, out of place.

Sheila went into a bedroom and came out with some swatches of cloth, samples of the material that the bridesmaids' dresses were to be made from. "I thought we could take these with us tomorrow," she said.

Astrid was in the city to buy her clothes for the wedding and Sheila had offered to come shopping with her.

"They might help us to find something that would tone in," Sheila said.

Astrid hadn't known that she would be expected to tone in. If it had been up to her, she would have got a navy suit and a pink blouse, because that was the kind of thing she liked, and she could get a lot of wear out of it later. Now she understood that this would not do.

"The mothers of the bride and groom have to be in coordinating colors," Sheila said.

Astrid nodded. "Whatever you think," she said.

Astrid did not think of her son's wedding as something that she might enjoy, but as something that—if she was lucky—she might succeed in fitting into. Usually when she attended a wedding it was as a spectator and she was happiest when she thought of herself that way at this one: as a spectator. Even the fact that she would have a better seat than usual was something that she didn't like to dwell on.

"I don't suppose it matters very much what *I* wear," Astrid said now, meaning it as a joke. "Nobody will be looking at *me*."

She expected Sheila to smile and say, "Oh, go on," but Sheila didn't do that. Instead her face took on a very cool look —a *city* look, Astrid thought—and she spoke as if from a conscious distance. "We *do* want things to be nice," she said.

Astrid was taken aback. "Okay for you," she thought. "Okay for you." But she was too intimidated by the whole situation to put very much heart into it. She told herself that putting on this wedding was a big job for Sheila, that it was a job she certainly wouldn't want dumped in *her* lap.

"It isn't as if we want anything elaborate or pretentious, you know," Sheila said. "I mean, those things don't *matter*, do they?"

Astrid did not answer. She had already observed that what Sheila thought mattered one time was not what she thought mattered another. Things were always changing with her. Take the matter of churches.

When plans for the wedding were first discussed, the ceremony was to have been held in a neighbourhood church. "That's where Roxanne went to Sunday School when she was just a little girl," Sheila said. Later, however, Sheila had found a church with red carpeting up the aisles, stained glass windows, a Gothic arch over the doorway. "A place like that looks so nice in the photographs," she said. And then, "We were lucky to get in there, you know."

Astrid, who had never been to either church, felt instinctively that she would have been more comfortable in the first. However, Sheila had also changed the place that the reception was to be held, and this change, to Astrid, seemed like an improvement. The reception was to include a dinner and dancing afterwards, and at first Sheila had planned to hold it in the Chateau Burgoyne, a downtown hotel that Astrid had never had occasion to enter, but which she thought of as being pretty high-toned. Later, however, Sheila had settled on the banquet room of a nice but less-imposing restaurant. "Those big, downtown hotels get booked up months ahead of time," Sheila said, as if explaining. But a minute later she lowered her voice as if she were afraid of being overheard, even though she and Astrid were the only people in the house. "Besides," she said, "it's one place where we can save a bit of money without having it show too much."

That was the thing about Sheila, Astrid thought. You never knew where you were with her. What she said she wanted and what she really wanted could be two different things. What she was saying now was, "All we want is a nice, warm, *family* sort of occasion."

"It's not our side that wants all the fuss and feathers," Astrid felt like telling her.

"Our side" meant Astrid's brothers and sisters, her nieces and nephews, all of whom would be at the wedding.

Astrid felt an eldest sister's pride in her family. "There's a lot worse people around," is the way she would have put it. There was nothing put-on about any of her family, a fact in which Astrid felt pride, and nothing demanding about them either. They took what they were offered and made the best of it. If it wasn't good enough, well, it was the offerer who ought to be ashamed of that. They were people who knew how to behave themselves, Astrid thought.

It sometimes seemed to Astrid that her family were just

about the only people around any more who thought about things as she did.

"The caterer says he can serve lunch at midnight if we want it," Sheila said.

Astrid liked the sound of that. That was the way things were done in her family: a cup of coffee and a bite to eat at the end of an evening. It was a way of saying, "Glad you could come. Come again." Not to have offered such hospitality would have seemed niggardly, she thought.

Astrid imagined herself joining her family for the midnight lunch. It would be the best part of the wedding, she thought: the day over and all of them free to let down and enjoy themselves a little.

"That sounds real nice," she said.

"Good," Sheila said. "Then I think we'll have that."

It made Astrid feel good to think about the midnight lunch, but her feeling good did not last long, because Sheila began to talk about the order that people were to walk in and stand in and speak in—entering the church, standing in the receiving line, responding to toasts. She spoke of processionals and recessionals. From time to time she consulted her wedding books to make sure that she had everything right.

Astrid did not ask why they had to do these things, seemingly so foreign to them all. She accepted that these things had to be, the way that children accept the visits of a school inspector. Such talk made her feel humble, inadequate, but she accepted that too.

"I just hope I don't do anything to spoil things," she said later that night when she was back at Sophie's, sitting in Sophie's kitchen and drinking instant coffee.

"Spoil things!" Sophie said. "How could you spoil things?" But she spoke with the extra energy that people give their speech when what they want to tell you is that they don't know what you are talking about.

Astrid smiled, grateful for Sophie's support.

"It seems to me it would be easy," she said.

Shopping the next day turned out to be more involved than Astrid had expected. She had thought that she and Sheila would go to some store, look over the dresses and then pick out whichever dress seemed best to them. But Sheila went at things differently. For Sheila, shopping was a matter of starting out with a particular dress in mind and then tramping from store to store until you found it.

What she was looking for, she said, was a silky print with apricot and rust tones in it. But when the first store turned out to have nothing in Astrid's size that matched that description, Sheila insisted that Astrid try on what they did have. "You never know," she said.

From then on, the day was unpleasant for Astrid. There was a succession of fitting-rooms in which the fluorescent lighting seemed always to be flickering. There was a succession of clerks, all of whom addressed their remarks to Sheila, even though they knew it was Astrid who was buying the dress. There was a succession of dresses, each of which Sheila studied, head to one side, and then finally rejected.

"It got pretty tiresome," Astrid imagined herself telling Sophie later.

When a beautiful dress finally did come along, it seemed to Astrid that it was a miracle that she was still able to recognize that fact. She pulled a blue and white silk dress down over sticky shoulders and quite suddenly saw in the mirror a thing of beauty.

The dress fitted as if it had been made with her in mind. It had a soft neckline, a nice easy skirt and three-quarter length sleeves, which was the length that Astrid liked. But to try to sum up the dress by describing neckline, skirt, sleeves, would be like trying to sum up a hyacinth by describing petals, pistil, stamen. Some dresses have elegance, integrity, perfection; some don't. This one did and Astrid knew it at once. She knew that if she bought this dress, she would look as good as she possibly could look at Billy's wedding. More than that, it seemed to her that in this dress, she would know how to *act*.

The knowledge, however, far from removing her problems, gave her new ones. Just *because* she liked the dress so much, she knew that she couldn't buy it unless somebody could prove to her that she ought to have it.

There was a situation that kept recurring in Astrid's life. Often when she was going into some new situation, she would be afraid that she wouldn't know what to wear or how to conduct herself. Then, as if by magic, the answer would be revealed to her. But then she would find herself powerless to act upon it.

There was a part of Astrid that wanted that dress, that wanted to strut a little, to let people see, just for once, how good she *could* look. But there was another part of her that wasn't willing to stand out in any way, that drew back from the idea that she might look like she was trying to be somebody.

Not to look good enough for the wedding? Or to risk looking *too* good? Astrid felt paralyzed between the choices. It seemed to her that she couldn't take personal responsibility for deciding the matter in her own favour. If she was to buy this dress and enjoy having done it, somebody else would have to talk her into it.

"This dress doesn't look too bad," she said to Sheila, keeping her voice casual.

Sheila studied it for a moment, head tilted, considering. "The blue wouldn't tone in with the bridal party," she said finally.

It went against Astrid's principles to say another word. All the same, "I still kind of like it," she heard herself saying.

"It *is* pretty," Sheila said. She spoke as if reassuring a child.

"But think how it would look in the pictures," she said. "One blue among all the apricots and rusts."

Astrid decided then that she wasn't meant to have the dress, and took it off.

The dress they finally found was not at all like the blue one. It was sleeveless, which Astrid didn't like, and it had a sort of shawl affair sewn into the shoulder seams and knotted in the front. It was made of chiffon, printed in white, green and rust colors. It was because of the rust in the print that Sheila liked it. "It's just absolutely perfect," she said.

And so, although it cost a good deal more than she thought it should have, Astrid bought it. She wanted to get the job over with, to make her escape from the fitting-rooms. That, however, was not to be. Sheila felt that alterations were needed, and called for a seamstress.

"And while we're at it," she said to Astrid, "the dress would look a lot better if you got yourself a padded brassière."

She tilted her head to one side, studying Astrid. "I'll just ask the girl to bring one in," she said.

She was already moving toward the door when Astrid spoke. "Oh no you don't," she said.

Because suddenly it seemed to Astrid that the time had come to draw the line. If Sheila could suggest a thing like this —without even bothering to pretend any diffidence about it —it could only be because Sheila had been misjudging her. When Astrid went along with things, didn't demand that everything be done *her* way, it was because *she* had principles. It was not because she was someone who could be led around by the nose, which was what Sheila seemed to think. The sooner that Sheila realized this, the better. *She* might not know everything there was to know about putting on weddings, Astrid told herself, but she did know one thing. She wasn't going to stand around at her son's wedding and have people eye her up and down and speculate about changes in her silhouette.

"I'm not wearing a padded bra," she said.

"Don't be silly," Sheila said. "Lots of people wear padded bras nowadays. Nobody thinks anything of it."

"*I* do," Astrid said.

"The *idea*!" Sophie said when Astrid told her about it later. "The *very idea*!"

"I just felt that enough was enough," Astrid said.

"You should have told her a thing or two," Sophie said. "You should have just got up on your high horse and told her."

"I might do it yet," Astrid said. "If I take a notion to, I just might do it."

It gave them relief to talk this way. It made them feel like people who could speak up when they felt like it, like people who could be pushed so far and no further.

"You should take a page out of Sheila's book," Sophie said. "She certainly isn't backward about coming forward."

It was some time before Sophie remembered to ask Astrid about her dress.

"Oh, it's just a dress," Astrid said. "It will be good enough for me, I guess."

The day of the wedding, however, Astrid wasn't so sure. She looked in the mirror and saw a stranger, a woman with large, bare arms, whose neck was coarse-skinned, sun-reddened. It was the chiffon of the dress that made her look like this, Astrid realized. It was as if chiffon was a material that couldn't help itself; it had to point out that here was a woman who had no business to be got up this way.

It was the bareness of her arms that bothered her most. Astrid was conscious of them walking up the aisle before the ceremony started, and afterwards when people lined them up outside the church for snapshots. She was conscious of them at the reception, when dinner was followed by toasts that went on and on. Once dinner was out of the way, however, it seemed to Astrid that things were beginning to pick up a little.

Ordinarily, Astrid liked to go to parties. She didn't go for the non-stop talking that some people seemed to feel was necessary at any social occasion, nor for the dancing, but just to watch. She liked to find herself a good seat near the wall and settle back and watch whatever was going on. Often it gave her things to think about for days afterwards.

Her family was like she was. When the dancing began after dinner, Astrid looked across the hall and saw her sisters sitting all in a row, their arms folded across their chests and their hands tucked into the inner curve of their arms. There they sat, she thought: behaving themselves but enjoying themselves too.

To make sure that none of the family went home early, Astrid told them all about the lunch at midnight. "We wouldn't miss it," they said.

But when midnight came, no lunch appeared. At first Astrid didn't think very much about it, but when 12:30 came and there was still no sign of lunch, she began to feel uneasy. She went to look for Sheila.

"Lunch?" Sheila said, speaking quickly. "I thought we'd told you. We decided against lunch. We thought it might look—you know—*excessive*."

And that was that.

As Astrid turned to go back to her family's table, she felt the pressure of tears at the back of her eyes. She hadn't expected much of this wedding, but she had been counting on this. Only now that it had been taken from her did Astrid fully understand what this time was to have meant to her. In Astrid's mind, Billy's wedding still had not really taken place. It was to have been this time with her family, a time of joking and laughter, which was to have made it real to her.

It seemed to Astrid that she had asked nothing, had gone along with everything Sheila wanted. And then Sheila had gone and pulled a thing like this on her. Astrid thought that the years ahead looked bad for Billy, having to try to get along with the kind of people who could pull a thing like this.

She told her family. There was a moment's silence. Then the phrases of consolation began. "Nobody expects another thing," they told her. "Coffee would only keep us awake," they said. "We just got up from the supper table," they said. And, "Heavens, I can still taste the supper in my mouth." But Astrid wouldn't smile as they wanted her to.

"I feel bad," she said.

Sophie joined the others in declaring that lunch wasn't necessary, that lunch wasn't expected. But in the car driving home, she had other things to say. "Imagine her changing a thing like that without asking you," Sophie said. "That's what gets me."

"I guess the world is full of people who don't know how to act," Astrid said.

"It isn't as if they spared any expense when it came to other things," Sophie said. "When it came to clothes or flowers or anything you could take a picture of, the best was none too good for them."

"It's a funny way of looking at things, that's all I can say," Astrid said.

"The trouble with Sheila is that she wants to do what *she* wants to do," Sophie said.

Astrid didn't speak. She had started to feel the over-ness of the wedding. It hadn't turned out the way she wanted it to, but it was over with. And she had lived through it, she thought. That was something.

In the semi-darkness of the car, Astrid saw Sophie give her head a little shake, as if she were still trying to believe what had happened.

"It would go against my principles to pull a stunt like

that," Sophie said. "Change things without even asking you."

Astrid was beginning to feel very tired. "Well, you or I would have asked," she said. The anger had gone out of her, and she was aware only of weariness.

"The trouble is, some people don't have any principles," she said.

HOOKING THINGS

At first I thought that the house we were to live in was a mansion. It was two-storeyed, of red brick and it had white pillars around the verandah at the front and even a balcony upstairs.

The balcony opened off our part of the house. Also in our part of the house, were a bedroom and a sort of kitchen, a room furnished with a table, chairs, a Winnipeg couch and a washstand with an enamel dishpan on top. Water for the

77

dishpan was to be carried from a bathroom at the end of the hall.

There were no cooking arrangements visible at first glance but then my father opened the door to what had once been a clothes closet and we saw that the cookstove was in there. So were shelves for dishes and food.

There were four rooms in the upstairs of the house. Two of them belonged to other people, and two of them belonged to us: my father, my mother, my sister and me. The four of us would share the bathroom at the end of the hall with the people from the other upstairs rooms, but the people who lived downstairs had a bathroom of their own. My parents would sleep in the bedroom, and my sister and I would sleep in the kitchen, on the Winnipeg couch.

I do not remember that I found anything surprising about any of these arrangements. I had not had a bed to myself at home on the farm either. Indeed, at that stage of my life, I don't think that I knew that anyone did.

I sat down on the Winnipeg couch and looked around me. My parents were standing in the doorway, my father in his Air Force uniform, my mother in the new coat she had bought to ride on the train. She hadn't wanted to buy the coat—"I don't want people thinking I'm trying to be somebody," she had said—but she hadn't had anything else to wear and so she had had to.

It looked nice on her. She was looking around the room that was to be one-half of our home, but my father was looking at her. "I know airmen who have been looking for six months for a place to put their families," he said.

"I don't see anything the matter with this," my mother said. "This ought to be plenty good enough for us."

My father showed us the bathroom then, and the clothes closet, and we turned the electric lights on and off and opened and closed the dresser drawers.

"You girls will be wondering where there's a place to play," my father said, but he was wrong; I was wondering no such thing. I was thinking that if the people who lived in the other two upstairs rooms were to move away, we could have the second floor to ourselves. And if, after that, the people who lived downstairs moved away too, we could have the whole house to live in.

The whole *mansion*, I amended.

It was night-time when we arrived in Broadlands, so it was the next morning before I got my first good look at the city. I went out onto our balcony and what I saw astonished me.

Before me was a street on which every house was painted or stuccoed. There were no boards tacked to corners to hold up eavestroughing or balance rain-barrels. There were no milk pails overturned to air on fenceposts, no scrub rags spread to dry on fences. Where I came from, most houses had never been painted and had weathered to the colour of dark pewter. Here there was not even one house like that.

On this street, every house was set in its own square of green and the grass, like the houses, was perfect, every blade exactly like the blade next to it. The grass was also greener than the grass back home. Darker. Caragana hedges, so perfectly trimmed that they looked like green and growing boxes, ran around the lawns. They marched across the front of yards, turned corners smartly and then marched down the sides. I had never seen anything like it. It looked like the Emerald City of Oz.

I thought of the way things were where I came from, and the way things were here, and it seemed to me that a mistake had been made. I shouldn't have come from there; I should have come from here.

Then, as I watched, someone turned on a lawn sprinkler, and patterns of spray arose, like silvery sculptures in the morning air. Houses, lawns and now lawn sprinklers! *These things had been here all the time,* I thought, *and I hadn't known anything about them.*

Today I wouldn't call Broadlands a city at all—it was scarcely more than a biggish town—but that is not the way it seemed to me then. Then it seemed to me to be a place where things were happening. There was a war on and in Broadlands you felt at the centre of it. There was an airbase and a Prisoner of War camp near the city, and the downtown streets were filled with uniforms, with airmen from many countries, with "vet guards," veterans of the first world war who had donned khaki again to guard at the Prisoner of War camp. And there was one street where you could go to watch truckloads of Germans go by. They, too, wore a sort of uniform—faded blue fatigues with big red patches on the back—but except for that they looked more like ordinary people than you would have expected.

Most of my time, of course, was not spent uptown or watching Germans, but in my own neighbourhood, getting acquainted with neighbourhood children. In the long summer evenings they gathered in schoolyards to play games of *Red Light* and *Prisoner's Base* and *Run Sheep Run*. It was during a game of *Run Sheep Run* that I first met Lorena Larkin.

Do you remember *Run Sheep Run*? It is the game in which everyone goes off together to hide, following a complicated route, so that when the leader returns to draw a map in the dust for the child who is *It* the map will be as misleading as possible. Custom decrees that every bend and circle of the route be recorded on the map, but custom also decrees that the scale shall be distorted and the direction falsified. *Run Sheep Run* is a game not meant to be won, and it was enormously popular.

One night I was hiding behind a caragana hedge—the players felt no obligation to stay together once the map was drawn—impatiently watching the child who was *It* circling around the goal. From behind a nearby lilac bush I heard a jeering voice. "Goal-sticker," it shouted. "Yellow-Belly, Green-Guts."

The taunts had the desired effect. The child who was *It* left the goal area and I saw my chance. But before I could move, a dark girl about my age appeared from behind the lilac bush. "Come on, gang!" she said to me—I was the only one there— and then I was racing in home-free on the heels of Lorena Larkin.

Lorena Larkin. Broadlands. Lorena means Broadlands to me, and Broadlands means Lorena. Lorena and I were never each other's best friends and were each other's bosom companions only intermittently, but when I think of Broadlands, it is Lorena I think of. Perhaps this is because Lorena was on hand when I took up several of the more important aspects of my life in Broadlands. One of them, surprisingly, was church-going.

I had never gone to church before we came to the city. There was no church to go *to* out in the country where I came from, but I needn't have gone in the city either if I hadn't wanted to. My parents' indifference to religion—their own or mine—was profound. "You don't have to believe in God to be a good Christian," my father liked to say.

Lorena's family weren't church-goers either but Lorena decided to attend a Vacation School being held that summer at Thurston United Church. "There's nothing else to do," she said. "God, what a dump this place is!"

I thought I would like Vacation School.

"No you won't," Lorena said. "Vacation School is boring. Vacation School is drippy."

I had never heard of *boring*. I had never heard of *drippy* either. I filed both away as useful words. But I still wanted to go to Vacation School.

"Well, there's nothing to stop you," Lorena said. "They let anybody in."

I liked Vacation School. The games we played there were as different from the games we played in the schoolyard at night as anything you can imagine. On the first morning we played a singing game called *The Grand Old Duke of York*. Players lined up in two rows in the churchyard and then took turns marching down the centre and around the outside, while singing:

> The Grand Old Duke of York,
> He had ten thousand men,
> He marched them up to the top of the hill,
> And he marched them down again.
> And when they were up, they were up,
> And when they were down, they were down,
> And when they were only half-way up,
> They were neither up nor down.

It was a game without winners or losers and I liked it.

Lorena did not. "It's drippy," she said. "It's a titty-bottle game."

"It's the song I like," I said defensively.

"If it's the song you like, I can teach you a better one than that," Lorena said.

We were on our way home from the church, taking a shortcut across an empty lot, and Lorena stopped walking to sing her song to me.

> Hitler...has just one big ball,
> Goering...has two, but very small,
> Himmler...has something similar,
> And Go-balls...has no balls at all.

I smirked, to let Lorena know that I knew what balls were, and also because I liked her song. I didn't like it better than the songs we had been singing at Vacation School—*Mr. Frog*

Went a-Courting and *Hole in the Bottom of the Sea* —but I did like it.

At Vacation School, we made things. We laced paper plates together with red yarn to make letter holders, and we strung necklaces out of macaroni. One day we made wall plaques out of plaster of Paris. We wet pictures that we had cut out of Christmas cards and put them face-down in plates or soup bowls that we had brought from home. Then we poured wet plaster of Paris over them and put a loop of string in the back so that we could hang them up when they dried.

These activities were supervised by a magnificent lady called Mrs. Rumbelow. On the first day, Mrs. Rumbelow wore a paddy green suit, with a spray of artificial flowers pinned at the bosom. She had dinner rings on her fingers, and her bobby pins had brilliants on them. On succeeding days she wore other vivid costumes, with other large sprays of artificial flowers.

But no description I can give of Mrs. Rumbelow's dress can convey the kind of impression she made on me. To me there was a quality of just-rightness about Mrs. Rumbelow, about everything she did. When she sang, she sang loudly, to show us how it should be done, and her singing claimed the space she was in. It was as if Thurston United Church *belonged* to Mrs. Rumbelow. Not even Mrs. McAskill, the minister's wife, seemed more at home there.

Mrs. McAskill, in any case, lacked Mrs. Rumbelow's glamour. I would have liked her to have it, since she was the minister's wife, but she didn't. Mrs. McAskill was old and thin, and she had thin, white hair. In those wartime years when women were supposed to look crisp and jaunty, Mrs. McAskill did not look crisp and jaunty. Her dresses were of some soft material not then in fashion and they were not vivid in colour like Mrs. Rumbelow's. When they were blue, they were blue-grey, when they were green, they were green-grey, when they were rose, they were rose-grey. And her voice was not robust like Mrs. Rumbelow's, but thin and faintly Scots-accented.

The day that we made wall plaques, Mrs. Rumbelow and Mrs. McAskill were both there. Mrs. McAskill came down the table where we were working, straightening pictures in the bottoms of plates, and Mrs. Rumbelow followed with a pitcher of wet plaster of Paris. "That looks like it might be part of your mother's dinner set," Mrs. McAskill said when she got to my plate.

It wasn't. It was a plate that had been in a box of assorted things that my mother had bought at an auction sale for a quarter. My mother didn't have a dinner set. But I felt that Mrs. McAskill expected me to say that it was, and so I did.

Mrs. Rumbelow, working nearby, lifted her eyes and looked at Mrs. McAskill, and I saw that I had said something wrong. People *shouldn't* send parts of their dinner set to church to make plaques in, Mrs. Rumbelow's look said. *They* wouldn't have done it.

Mrs. McAskill looked sorry she had spoken and when she spoke again her voice was quick with concern and kindness. "Your mother must have wanted you to make a really nice plaque," she said reassuringly, and I found that her interpretation did make me feel better. Then she asked me to tell her my name again and said how nice it was to have so many new children coming to church, and asked me if my father was in the Air Force, and told me to bring my parents to church with me some time.

When Vacation School ended, there was an Achievement Day, at which we were to sing the songs we had learned and display the things we had made, and our parents were invited. But when I took the hectographed invitation home with me, my mother took it from me gingerly and held it by its edges between thumb and forefinger as she read it. Then she handed it to my father.

"I wonder what *they*'re after," she said.

My father read it. "I don't know," he said. "But you can bet your life there'll be a collection."

I felt myself grow hot. I had acquired from my reading some notion of the kind of things that parents were supposed to say, of the kind of people they were supposed to be. My reading had given me a standard to judge parents by and it grieved me that my own so regularly fell below it.

"You don't have to come," I told them. "I can go by myself." What I meant was: "You don't have to come to anything with me ever."

My parents accepted my announcement with relief and I was relieved that they did. If they were going to think inappropriate things and behave in inappropriate ways, I didn't want them around the church. I could, I felt, be inappropriate enough all by myself.

I began to attend not only Sunday School but church. I liked both. I liked sitting by myself in a pew at the back on summer Sundays and watching the church fill with ladies in summer dresses, with men in suits, with children in newly-polished shoes. The ladies would settle themselves, spreading their skirts under them, and then take off their gloves very carefully, one finger at a time. They were not ladies you could imagine in slumber nets or hair-curlers or fur-lined bedroom slippers. Mrs. Rumbelow would enter the church, seat herself at the organ and begin to play, the flowers on her bosom fluttering softly. Then the minister would come in and the service would begin.

Mr. McAskill, the minister, was a sort of male equivalent of Mrs. McAskill—he too was thin and old and had thin, white hair—and it seemed to me that he matched his wife as a salt shaker matches a pepper shaker. Winter and summer he wore a knitted maroon jerkin between his layers of clerical black, and he had a preaching style that my father—who had once heard him at a compulsory church parade on the airbase

—described as "whiney."

I liked Mr. McAskill's preaching style. It was one of the things that made Thurston United Church what it was, and I liked everything about Thurston United Church. I liked the oak pews, smelling faintly of lemon oil, and the Boston ferns in matching oak fernstands. I liked the brass collection plates, padded with green felt so that coins wouldn't make an unseemly noise. I liked the light that came through the windows and, outside, the cottonwood trees, heavy in leaf. I liked the way that people stood up and cleared their throats before singing *Holy, Holy, Holy* at the beginning of service.

Once a month there was a Communion service. Trays of grape juice, grooved at the bottom to hold special little grape juice glasses, were passed along the pews and you helped yourself. There was a shelf on the back of the pew in front of you, grooved to hold your glass when you were finished with it. Everything fitted; everything had its place. I liked this orderliness and the sense it gave me that things were happening as they should. My life outside the church at that time was by no means orderly.

I had not known, for example, how difficult it would be to live in so little space. On the farm space was not a thing I had thought about or wanted. It was simply a thing that was there when I needed it. But living in a cramped apartment I came to long for even some semblance of privacy. I remember at one point deciding that I could be perfectly happy if only I could have a box with a lock on it. I had seen such a box in a store uptown. It was made of varnished red cedar and it was filled with writing paper. On the front was a small brass lock no bigger than your thumbnail.

"What would you want a thing like that for?" my mother asked when I told her that I did.

I wanted it to put things in.

"What things?" my mother asked.

I didn't know. The things I already had wouldn't do; other

people had already seen them. But when I got new things, I would put *them* in there.

This was not a thing I could explain to my mother, who had her suspicions about things like locked boxes and closed doors. She equated locking things away with a kind of miserliness, I think, but she also felt that to even *want* to lock a box or close a door was a sign that something was wrong.

"What's the matter with you?" she would ask when I demanded some privacy. "What have you got that you don't want the rest of us to see?"

Now I think that my need for seclusion was a thing she really did not understand. She was a different kind of person than I was. The object of living, as far as she was concerned, was to be able to be completely open, to be the kind of person who could say, "*I* have nothing to hide."

My mother wanted my sister and me to be open too, and she thought that the way to achieve this was to question us. "What did you want to go and do that for?" she was always asking us. "What's the matter with you anyway?"

It seemed to me that my mother's eyes missed nothing. Lorena could pull off all sorts of things right under her mother's nose while I trembled and waited for the roof to fall in, but Mrs. Larkin never seemed to be aware that anything was going on. I envied Lorena her absent-minded mother. Even back on the farm I had envied children whose parents were less interested in them than my parents were in me. But since we had come to the city, it seemed to me that my parents' scrutiny had become even closer.

"What are you up to now?" my mother was always asking me. "What are you trying to get away with?"

I never had any answer for her. I had not yet learned to explain myself and the demand that I do so confused and debilitated me. Often I ended up in tears.

It was then that I missed the farm. On the farm, you could run outside and fling yourself on the ground and weep, knowing that nobody could tell you to "Straighten up and be quick about it." You might not be happy but at least you could be alone. There were lots of places on the farm for that. Here there was no such place.

I was also, that summer, having problems in my friendship with Lorena. When we first came to Broadlands, Lorena and I had spent all our time together and I had supposed that we were going to be best friends. But then one day I went out to play and found Lorena with a girl I had never seen before. Her name was Peggy Todd and she looked like Lorena. Both of them were tall and dark and wiry, while I was short and fair and pudgy. Peggy had been away on a holiday with her family, Lorena told me, but now she was back. She and Peggy were each other's best friends and always had been. "We started school at the same time," she said. "In the same room and on the same day." She made it sound like an event of historic, even mystical, significance.

Three can be an awkward number in friendships, even for adults. If two are on the inside track, then one is not. But if I knew that then, it was knowledge I rejected. Lorena and Peggy were each other's best friends. I, too, wanted a best friend, and it did not occur to me that the best place to look for one was not in an already existing relationship. I think I felt, as perhaps all hangers-on do, that all I had to do was hang around long enough and I would become like the hung-on-to, like Lorena and Peggy. Both of them. It seemed to me a not impossible ambition, to become Lorena-and-Peggy. I planned to be methodical about it: to make a study of them and then appropriate their qualities.

In Broadlands that summer, girls my age wore a garment called a playsuit. It was a short one-piece garment a little like a bathing suit. Lorena and Peggy both had them. I did manage to persuade my mother to get me one, but when she brought it home, it was the wrong kind. Lorena's and Peggy's playsuits had skirts on the bottom of them, while mine looked like shorts, and I felt the difference keenly. It was as if their skirts somehow invalidated my playsuit.

Another thing that troubled me was that Lorena and Peggy got allowances and I did not. I had never heard of an allowance before we came to the city but now that I had heard of them, I wanted one.

My mother gave me spending money but I could not persuade her to give it to me in the form of an allowance. I think that she felt that to give a fixed sum every week would be to imply that the child was *entitled* to receive it, and she didn't like the idea that children might feel entitled to things. "Just because Lorena and Peggy have something doesn't mean that you have to have it too," she said.

Sometimes I went places with Lorena and Peggy, and sometimes I got left behind. The city was surrounded by prairie, and Lorena and Peggy could get on their bicycles and ride out of town, past the last street of houses, past snow-fences choked with tumbleweed, through the river valley and into the hills beyond. "See you," they would say, and then I would watch them pedalling away, their wheelspokes glinting in the sun.

Even after I got my own bicycle I couldn't join them, because I couldn't learn to ride. I'd start to ride and then I'd feel myself falling, so I'd stop riding to keep from falling.

So I hit on a scheme. It seemed to me that the thing to do was to learn to ride gradually, by easy stages. There was a porch railing along the back of our house and I would get my bike and ride alongside of that, holding on to the railing with one hand. It seemed to me that bike-riding was a skill that you could sneak up on, that one day I would find out that I *had* learned to ride, without ever having had to let go first.

Unable to ride a bike, I found myself drawn more and more into the life of the church, and it was not, I think, *only* a desire to belong that drew me there. One day at Sunday School Mrs. McAskill asked me to go into the church to get a songbook that she had left on the organ. I trotted out of the Sunday School room and into the church, happy to have been asked, but just inside the door, I stopped. There was a feeling in that room that I had not experienced before. There was space there, and there was silence. I was alone. It occurred to me that it was the first time I had been alone in that much space since we had come to Broadlands.

I felt a need to expand into the space, to fill it somehow. It was as if there was something in it that was calling to me, some presence. I would not, I think, have been surprised to see angels.

But though I could feel the room asking something of me, I could think of nothing to do. If people said prayers in a church when there was no service going on, it was an activity I had never heard of.

Finally I remembered Mrs. McAskill's songbook, got it and left. But the feeling I had in that room felt real, and it stayed with me.

It stayed with me even after I took up the next interest of my life in Broadlands, which was shoplifting. "Hooking things," we called it.

Peggy had to help her mother take care of her little brother on Saturdays, so Lorena spent Saturdays with me. We would walk up Twelfth Street to the Lealta Theatre, or uptown to the Roxy to see the latest double bill, and then we would head on to the Metropolitan store for a hot dog and root beer. The Metropolitan was *our* store. We bought our hot dogs there and we hooked things there. We wouldn't have thought of hooking anything at Eaton's.

But the Metropolitan! Oh, the Metropolitan! What a world of wonders that store was in those days!

The Metropolitan had everything. It had confetti for weddings and icebox flowers for corsages. It had perfume bottles shaped like roses and pink satin slippers with wedgie heels. It had kerchiefs printed with Churchill's face and kerchiefs printed with London Bridge. It had maple-leaf brooches and V-for-Victory brooches and brooches that said *There'll Always be an England*. It had framed pictures of English country cottages nearly smothered in lupines and pictures with verses addressed *To My Sweetheart* and *To My Wife* and *To Mother, the Queen of My Heart*. It had satin cushions similarly decorated, and one cushion on which there was a picture of pioneers and their covered wagon, and underneath, a verse which said: *The Spirit grows with its allotted Spaces. The Mind is narrow'd in a narrow sphere.*

The Metropolitan had dresser scarves, stamped for embroidery with pictures of hoop-skirted southern belles and Bluebirds of Happiness. It had crêpe paper, which was used by energetic ladies to make artificial flowers. The first Cala lilies I ever saw, and the first daffodils, and the first American Beauty roses, were all made of Dennison's Double Weight Crêpe Paper.

The Metropolitan also had flowers that were not just potential, but actual. It had silk flowers like the ones that Mrs. Rumbelow wore pinned to her chest. It was a revelation to me to find out that these things could be *bought*, that for 59¢ or even 39¢, you could turn your mother into a reasonable facsimile of Mrs. Rumbelow.

It had fancy underwear, which was called lingerie. There were satin slips trimmed with lace, and panties that came in many colours and were embroidered with the names of the days of the week, so you would remember to change them. In those elastic-less days of wartime, the panties fastened at the waistline with buttons.

The Metropolitan had goldfish. It had wax fruit: pears and apples and peaches and cherries. I could imagine them piled into a bowl in the centre of Mrs. Rumbelow's dining-room table. It had coloured candles and glass candle-holders. It had Blondex shampoo, used by ladies who wanted to keep their hair from getting dark but who didn't want to be bleached blondes. It had bath salts and Evening in Paris perfume. It had fingernail buffers. *Fingernail buffers!* One could scarcely imagine a life gracious enough to contain all these things.

In a back corner of the store, where the smell of oilcloth was strong, there were framed pictures of movie stars for sale. I used to spend hours looking at them, trying to decide whose picture I would buy if I had the money. Would I choose Betty Grable or Dianna Lynn? Jennifer Jones or June Allyson? John Hodiak or Dennis Morgan or Turhan Bey? I didn't know then that people bought these pictures for the *frames*; I took it for granted that anyone would want a picture of a movie star.

At the cosmetic counter, you could buy the lipstick that made Ginger Rogers look like Ginger Rogers, the cold cream that made Esther Williams look like Esther Williams. I knew that this was so because the packages said so. There was also a preparation called *Stillman's Freckle Cream*, which was said to cure both freckles and pimples. None of the movie stars admitted to using it but I would have been willing to give it a try, even without their endorsement.

Certain merchandise in the Metropolitan, precious things like zircon rings and identification bracelets and Waterman fountain pens, were not displayed on open counters but were kept under glass, so that you could not handle them without asking a clerk. I used to feel uncomfortable around those covered counters, as if someone was watching me.

Lorena was the first of us to hook anything. One day after we had left the Metropolitan she held out her hand and unclenched her fist to reveal a small brooch, a brass maple leaf covered with ruby brilliants. "See what I got," she said.

"Where did that come from?" I asked.

"I hooked it," Lorena said. And then, "It was lying right on the edge of the counter. It could have fallen off." People should take better care of their things, she meant.

As I looked at it lying in her hand, a most extraordinary

feeling came over me. It was as if ceilings were rising and horizons were moving back.

"Don't you want to go back and see if you can't hook something too?" Lorena asked.

I felt as if I did. And I didn't. It seemed to me that what Lorena had done was brave, and I felt as if I could be brave too. At the same time there was a feeling that I couldn't define, a feeling that said *maybe not*. What I finally decided was to go back into the store and let myself be tempted. Perhaps I would withstand the temptation.

Back in the store I found myself standing in front of a display of little white Scottie dogs. They were made of plaster, the kind that glistens like pressed salt, and they had little bottles of perfume tied to their necks with bits of plaid ribbon. They were the kind of thing that you gave to people for their birthdays, or if you drew their name at Christmas.

The Scottie dogs were small. Not too big—not *much* too big—to hide in the palm of your hand. It occurred to me that if I had not had a hot dog and a root beer, I would have had almost enough money to buy one.

I was standing in front of the Scottie dogs thinking this. And then a Scottie dog was in my pocket. It was almost as if he had needed a hiding place and I had provided it for him.

I felt good. There was, however, the problem of what to do with the Scottie dog. I couldn't take it home; there was no place to hide it. And I would have to get rid of it before I could hook anything else.

It was already clear to me that that was what I was going to do: keep on hooking things. It might have been Lorena's idea to hook something in the first place but it was definitely my idea to keep on doing it. And *why* I wanted to do it—take things that I didn't need and couldn't use, couldn't even brag about having—is a total mystery to me today.

Sometimes I stole lipsticks. I would come out of the latest Jennifer Jones movie at the Roxy and head across the street to

the Metropolitan and steal the lipstick I would have needed if
I had been Jennifer Jones and heading off to a meeting with
Joseph Cotton. Then I would walk home and, someplace
along the way, dig a hole and bury the lipstick. I buried it not
as a dog buries a bone, with at least the possibility of later
retrieval, but to be done with it, to put it behind me. And it
was important that it be hidden, buried. I couldn't just drop
it, leave it exposed to view.

I suppose that compared to things like the lipsticks, the
birthday cake decorations made a kind of sense. There were
roses, doves and letters that spelled out HAPPY BIRTHDAY,
all made of a kind of ossified icing. They were packaged in
cellophane-topped boxes, and it was possible to puncture the
cellophane with a thumbnail, palm a letter or a dove, and
then eat it in another part of the store.

Often when I got to the counter where the decorations
were sold, I would find that someone had been there before
me. There would be boxes on which the cellophane was
already punctured, from which decorations had already been
removed. I think now that the clerks left these boxes there in
the belief that, if children had to pilfer, they might as well do
it from packages that were already unsaleable. I stayed away
from those damaged boxes. They were not as they should have
been and I was afraid of them. I always broke my own cellophane, began my own box.

How did it happen that we were never caught? Was shoplifting something we were terribly, terribly good at? I don't
know. But I do know that I didn't worry much about getting
caught. I had the conviction in those years that I was, if not
invisible, then at least unrecognizable. When I met people I
knew uptown, I never knew whether to speak to them or not,
because I was quite sure that they couldn't recognize me.
Perhaps this aberration gave me a feeling of security.

And I *did* feel secure shoplifting. In fact, when I look back,
it seems to me that just about the only time in those years

when I didn't feel anxiety was when I was in the Metropolitan store, filling my pockets with things that didn't belong to me.

Lorena tired of shoplifting before I did. We were on our way uptown one Saturday when she told me. Hooking things was drippy, she said; it was a titty-bottle thing to do. She meant to lay off.

"You mean for keeps?" I said. "Never hook anything again?"

"Well, not after today," Lorena said. "Today can be our Quits Day."

That day I stole a wedding ring. It may have been made of brass but I can't be sure of that. It looked like any other wedding ring. And that day, instead of burying it, I decided to take my prize home.

I knew that there was no place in our rooms that I could hide it where it wouldn't be found, so I decided to invent a story to explain having it. I told my mother that I had been walking along when I saw a handkerchief in the mud beside the sidewalk. I had gone to investigate and then I had seen the ring beside it. I had left the handkerchief there, I said primly, because it was dirty.

Strangely, my mother did not question my story. She called Mrs. Rooney, the woman who lived in the downstairs of our house, to come upstairs, and then she got me to repeat it.

Mrs. Rooney nodded her head from time to time as I spoke, and the metal wave-clips set in her hair in parallel rows glistened in the light. "It'll be some married woman stepping out on her husband, I bet," she said. "Her husband is probably overseas and she's carrying on with somebody...one of those vet guards, more than likely."

My mother shook her head, as if to say there were all kinds of people in the world.

"Probably she had her ring off so people wouldn't know she was married," Mrs. Rooney said. "She'd have it in her pocket so she could quick slip it on if she ran into anyone she knew. Then she reached into her pocket for her hankie and the ring came out too," she said.

I could almost see it happening.

"The handkerchief had the letter *M* embroidered in one corner," I said, seized with sudden inspiration.

"The letter *M*!", Mrs. Rooney said. She sounded indignant, and I waited for her interpretation of this, but I should have kept my mouth shut. My speaking reminded my mother that I was there.

"Why don't you go out and play?" she said. "Why don't you ride your bike?"

So I left my mother and Mrs. Rooney and went downstairs to my bicycle. As I pedalled back and forth holding on to the porch railing I thought of the woman and the vet guard and the wedding ring. And then I thought about Lorena and the Metropolitan and our Quits Day. And then the tears began to drip down my cheeks. It seemed to me that all my future was behind me, that I had nothing to look forward to anymore.

I don't know how long it was before the idea occurred to me that just because Lorena was quits didn't mean that I had to be. I had said I was but I was under no obligation to keep my word. All I had to do was find a new partner—you couldn't hook things alone—and I could go on as before.

And that is what I did. I found a new partner. And when that partner tired of hooking things, I found another. And then another.

All this time, my life in Thurston United Church was going on as usual. I had a child's ability to be only one person at a time, and thoughts of the Metropolitan never rose to trouble me when I was around the church, which was a good deal of the time.

On Tuesday afternoons after school, I went to meetings of something called the Mission Band. Meetings of this group opened by reciting a poem:

Girls, girls, with pigtails and curls,
Where are you going today?
Oh we are going to Mission Band,
To learn the news of many lands.

Then we sang a song that concluded with the words:

Happy, happy children,
Pretty butterflies,
Aren't you glad God made us,
To delight your eyes?

Mission Band was a sort of mid-week Sunday School for pre-adolescent girls. Older girls went to CGIT—Canadian Girls in Training—and boys went to Scouts or Tuxis.

Probably my life in the church and my life in the Metropolitan would have continued on separate tracks forever if it hadn't been for the Mission Band money-boxes.

In Mission Band, each of us was given a cardboard box, a small yellow cube decorated on the sides with pictures of little black children in Africa. There was a slit on the top of the box and you were supposed to put a few pennies into it every week, presumably to do something for the little children in Africa. I and a girl called Joanie Tyler were given the job of putting the Mission Band boxes away into a cupboard in the kitchen after every meeting.

It was Joanie who observed that the slits on the top of some of the boxes were too wide. "Money could fall out of them," she said disapprovingly.

We looked at each other.

Then we turned the boxes upside down and money did

come out of them.

"People should be more careful," Joanie said.

And then we made some other slits wider and money came out of them too.

There was a Chinese confectionery across the street from the church. We took to going to it after Mission Band meetings, treating ourselves to twin popsicles and Sundae Sticks and Cuban Lunches and Sweet Sixteen gum. It did not occur to us that we might have been smarter to spend our money out of sight of the church, that having so much spending money might strike people as suspicious, but that was all right because it did not occur to the church people either. The church people were, in fact, a remarkably unsuspicious lot.

If I had understood that, if I had been able to believe that unsuspicious people existed, I probably never *would* have been caught. But I didn't understand it. I took it for granted that people watched for things to happen and that the best way to be in the clear when a crime was discovered was to be the one to report it. And that is what Joanie and I did. We told the Mission Band leader that money was missing from *our* boxes.

"Are you sure, girls?" the leader asked, looking very grave.

We said that we were sure. "I put a dime in my box last week and it's not there now," I said. "I know because I shook all my money out and counted it."

She told us not to say anything about it to anyone, that she would look into it, and we put the boxes away again. Then we headed across the street to the Chinaman's.

Ah, me. The meetings that must have gone on, the solemn consultations. I could not imagine them then, but I can imagine them now. Everyone would want to find some way to help us; everyone would want to do the right thing.

I have no way of knowing what sorts of alternatives were considered, but I do know what the good people of Thurston United Church finally decided to do. They decided to have

Mr. McAskill preach a sermon. About stealing. About how stealing was wrong.

Mr. McAskill was not a young man. If it had not been for the war, which had taken so many of the younger clergy out of civilian life, he would have been retired. He could have been putting his stamp collection in order, or writing letters to the editor, or growing roses on Vancouver Island. Instead he still had charge of a church, a church in a town that was bursting at the seams. And when a problem arose in his flock, he coped with it the best he knew.

I do not remember many of the sermons that Mr. McAskill preached during the time I attended his church, but I do remember that one. What Mr. McAskill said was that stealing was wrong, that people didn't feel good when they took things that didn't belong to them. He said that they thought they were going to feel good, but they didn't. And then they didn't know what to do about it.

I was sitting in my usual pew near the back of the church when Mr. McAskill began to speak, and I knew at once that his words were meant for me. A banner dropped from the ceiling announcing the fact could not have made it any clearer. He did not *look* at me, but I knew he was speaking to me. I felt that everyone must know it. I half expected people to turn in their pews to look at me.

Mr. McAskill began to speak of the agonies of remorse that people felt when they had done something wrong. I suppose it was part of his conception of human nature that people *would* feel agonies of remorse, but I don't remember that I ever did. But as Mr. McAskill began to describe it, I began to feel it. It was as if I were becoming the child he imagined me to be, a child somehow related to my usual church self: a child who wanted not only to be good, but never to have been bad in the first place.

When you had done something wrong, Mr. McAskill said, you had to make it right. And then he told a story to show

how this could be done.

Mr. McAskill's story was about a boy in his congregation, "now grown up and a respectable businessman in this city," who had once stolen some small thing from a store. The boy had acted on impulse, he said, taking something he coveted, expecting to enjoy it. But then he had been overcome by remorse and, after much suffering, had told Mr. McAskill of his trouble.

"There is only one thing you can do," Mr. McAskill said he had told the boy. "Only one thing that will make you feel better. You will have to make it right."

And so, at Mr. McAskill's direction, the boy had gone to the manager of the store he had stolen from and confessed his theft. And the manager had been so impressed with the boy's courage and truthfulness that he had given him a job, so that he could earn the money to pay for the thing he had taken. This had also, incidentally, launched the boy on his successful business career.

As Mr. McAskill was speaking, I tried his story on myself. I imagined myself in the Metropolitan Store. At the back, there was an open stairway that led to a sort of mezzanine, where the offices were located. I imagined myself walking along an aisle toward that stairway, past the fingernail buffers and the Blondex, past the cushion covers and movie stars. I saw myself climbing the stairs, saw the manager's door in front of me. I tried to see myself knocking at that door, tried to imagine myself entering, tried to picture myself telling the manager about all the things I had stolen.

And I knew I couldn't do it. What would the manager say when I told him? Wouldn't he want to see the things I had taken? I saw myself leading the manager around town, excavating lipsticks and perfume bottles. It was quite a lot to ask of a girl who was afraid to let go of the porch railing when she rode her bicycle.

Looking back today, it occurs to me that probably even Mr.

McAskill would not have expected *that* of me. It is only now, thinking about it, that I realize: *Mr. McAskill didn't know anything about the Metropolitan. Mr. McAskill was talking about Mission Band boxes.*

I suppose he thought his story would give me courage. If the boy in his story could confess to a store manager, whom he didn't know, I could confess to Mr. McAskill, whom I did. Mr. McAskill was trying to make it easy for me. He was trying to help.

A minister must fail often.

Not only did I not confess my misdemeanours to Mr. McAskill; once the terror of the sermon had faded, I went right on committing them.

But perhaps his sermon had an effect on me after all, because some time during that second summer in Broadlands, I *did* finally quit hooking things. I didn't have a Quits Day or anything like that; I just found one day that I *had* quit.

My life by then had new pleasures. My mother had got a job and when I came home it was often to an empty house. I could read or play with paper dolls in blessed solitude. And I had finally learned to ride the bicycle. I had accepted the fact that if you want to ride you have to go fast instead of slow, you have to move surely instead of tentatively...and you have to let go of the porch railing. Once I had made up my mind to that, it was easier than I expected it to be. It wasn't necessary to be brave incessantly, I discovered; once or twice would do it for all time.

And being able to ride the bicycle was like getting out of jail. I spent long days on the prairie west of town, where space was a thing that had no end.

Today when I look back, I find myself feeling a quite surprising amount of affection for the people of Thurston United Church, and for Mr. and Mrs. McAskill. For Mr. McAskill, especially. He was so decent, so game about trying: that tired, upright old man.

If there were a way of writing letters to people surely dead, I think I might write one to him, to tell him that I had gone straight, that I did finally stop hooking things. I would have liked him to know that. But I could no more tell him that I had stopped hooking things than I could tell him that I was hooking them in the first place, and without me telling him, there was no way he could know. You see, that fall I moved up from Mission Band into CGIT. And in CGIT we didn't have any money boxes.

A PAILFUL
OF PARTRIDGES

There are people that other people like to talk about. There is
an excitement about them, or a secret we want to know, and
we tell stories about them, trying to understand, to explain,
to get closer. My mother's cousin, Ellen Wheeler, was not
that kind of person.

Once, though, after she moved to the city, Ellen got her
name in the paper. She was getting off a city bus when she
caught her foot on the step. The doors closed and the bus

started up, but fortunately it stopped again before Ellen was seriously hurt.

The account in the paper did not tell where Ellen was going, nor where she had been, nor even where she came from, and these were serious omissions from my mother's point of view. "They should have said 'Mrs. Willard Wheeler, *formerly of Willow Bunch*,'" my mother said. "Or else *Mrs. Wheeler, the former Ellen Lockerbie.*' There could be any number of Mrs. Willard Wheelers in a place the size of Edmonton."

Uncle Nathan, who was staying on the farm with us, was sitting across the kitchen table from my mother, and he laughed. He knew that my mother was speaking out of a sort of delayed anxiety. Something terrible had almost happened to Ellen, and there was indignation, and you had to put it someplace.

"Maybe the paper thought it was the bus door that was interesting," my father suggested.

My mother looked up from the paper. "Don't be silly," she said. "A bus door could stand there until kingdom-come and nobody would get interested in it. It's the person getting stuck that's interesting."

It seemed to me that my mother had something there. It also seemed to me that if the telling of the story had been left up to my mother, it would have been a better story. It would have been vivid, rich in detail, and Ellen would not have been just a woman who got her foot stuck in a bus door, but a particular person, someone who mattered.

Uncle Nathan often smiled when my mother spoke, and he was smiling now. He enjoyed my mother's company a lot, in some ways more than my father did. Her stories, for instance. My mother was a born storyteller and Uncle Nathan relished her stories. My father did not.

My mother had stories about everyone, about people I knew and people I didn't know, about people who lived near Willow Bunch and people who had moved away. She had stories of people who took risks and squeaked through, and of people who played it safe and lost out. She had stories about which she said, "It was a near thing," meaning that tragedy had been averted by the merest chance, and stories of their opposite, of tragedies that ought never to have happened, but did.

Sometimes there were stories about *Maida*. Listening to these, I would feel more real, more significant, than my ordinary self. The things that happened to me meant something, I realized, more than I had known when they were happening, and I meant something too. Stories were told about me; therefore I existed.

If my mother enhanced things in her storytelling, it was not a thing that she did on purpose. It was her intention to tell you exactly what happened, no more and no less. She believed that you told stories to pass on what you had learned by your living, and that you had a responsibility to get things right. But she also liked the things that happened to mean something. "You'd wonder why these things would happen," she would say when the meaning wasn't clear to her. Or, "It makes no sense at all." She always sounded slightly aggrieved when she said this, as if life had a responsibility to make sense to her.

I am not sure what time of year it was when Ellen Wheeler got her foot stuck in the bus door. Probably it was summertime, since Uncle Nathan was staying with us. But it could also have been the Easter holidays. Uncle Nathan was a schoolteacher, a bachelor, and he spent his holidays from teaching on the farm with us. He didn't farm, exactly, although he still owned land. My father farmed Uncle Nathan's land and Uncle Nathan "helped out." Why he never found any other way to spend his summers and holidays was a question I never thought of asking.

"Does the paper say what kind of shoes Ellen was wearing?" Uncle Nathan asked.

My mother shook her head. The newspaper was on the kitchen table in front of her, and she had read the brief item several times, as if she hoped that new facts might have appeared between readings. "There's not a word about anything like that," she said.

"That shouldn't make any difference," my father said. "A bus ought to be safe no matter what kind of shoes you're wearing."

I was surprised to hear my father joining in the talk, the puzzling out of the story, such as this was. Storytelling ordinarily made him uneasy. "Some day you're going to find out something you don't want to know," he used to warn my mother, but I don't think that was really what troubled him. He just felt that silence was somehow *better* than speech. He didn't approve of giving too much away, didn't like people who were "windy." "The less said the better," he would say when even an innocent topic was being discussed. He listened to my mother's stories warily, nervous that something might get said that shouldn't get said. He was, however, interested in Ellen's mishap. Maybe it was because most stories are about people, about the things that happen between people, and it was this about them that made him uneasy. But this was different: what had happened here was strictly between Ellen and the bus door.

"I guess we'll have to wait until Ellen comes down to get the whole story," Uncle Nathan said.

"If we get it then," my mother said. "Ellen isn't much of a one to talk about herself."

That was true. What was also true was that if I had been given a choice, I would have preferred to get the story at secondhand from my mother, rather than at firsthand from Ellen. It would have been more interesting that way, and would probably also have seemed truer.

My mother had an extraordinary ability to evoke the reality of persons and events in her storytelling. She had only to say, "Now you take your Uncle Nathan," for Uncle Nathan to spring into mind, tall, good-looking and with a certain unmarried glamour. Uncle Nathan was fifteen years older than my father, and looked like him, only more so. Or she would say, "Now you take Mrs. Wheeler," and I would see that lady, Ellen's mother-in-law and our near neighbour. A sharp-eyed woman with a good figure and a firm walk, Mrs. Wheeler would have been rather handsome except for her nose, which was bent near the bottom like a periscope, so that she always gave the impression of heading around a corner.

Oddly enough, it was only when my mother said, "Now you take my cousin Ellen" that the picture that came to my mind was not a true one. Ellen had been my mother's best friend when they were both girls, and when my mother said, "Now you take Ellen," the Ellen who appeared to me was an intrepid girl, someone who tossed her curls a lot. The real Ellen, or at least the Ellen who came to visit us, was another person altogether. I look for her in my memory and what I find there is a faded woman, tired-moving and with no sense of season, someone forever sweltering in crepe in summer or shivering in rayon in winter.

For a long time, I think, I did not quite realize that the two Ellens were the same person, and when I did realize it, I marvelled that while I could see my mother's Ellen, she seemed unable to see mine.

"People used to say that Ellen was so shy and quiet," she would say, meaning back when they were girls. "But they never knew the mischief that went on behind those blue eyes." Or again, "Ellen was so pretty that people never realized what a devil she was."

Deviltry was a quality my mother admired.

And when my mother spoke of the grownup Ellen, the Ellen who came to visit us, she always spoke as if Ellen was the kind of person she was herself: quick-moving, restless, talkative. If she did notice Ellen's listlessness, she put it down as a temporary condition. "Ellen's not her old self this spring," she would say. Or "Ellen's a bit under the weather right now." She always sounded as if she expected things to get back to normal at any minute, as if she thought that when Ellen came to visit again, her footsteps would tap across the floorboards in time to the rapid, restless rhythm of my mother's own.

Ellen was a tired-moving woman, but she had an even more tired-moving husband. When I stayed at their place in the city, Willard would come home from work, have supper, maybe start to water the lawn, and then fall asleep on the chesterfield.

My mother could see *Willard's* lack of energy, but she put it down to city living. "What Willard needs is a few days in the country," she would say.

But when Willard came to visit us, he would spend his days collapsed on the Winnipeg couch in the kitchen. If he did get up to walk across the yard, he put you in mind of an old horse pulling a heavy stoneboat; it made you tired just to watch him.

When I was small, Willard didn't appeal to me—tired people don't usually appeal to children—but he didn't bother me either. Ellen did. When Ellen came to our house, I felt a kind of resentment. I thought of the Ellen in my mother's stories and I looked at the Ellen before me, and I felt cheated, as if a traitor had come. What I saw contradicted what I believed, and given a choice between seeing and believing, I would have taken believing every time.

Sometimes, after Willard and Ellen had gone back to the city, I would get out the chocolate box in which my mother kept her old snapshots. I liked looking at old pictures. I could spend hours over old pictures of my parents, pictures taken when they were young. I would look at their young faces and feel as if I had lived in their time, and known them. But after Ellen had been to see us, it was Ellen I wanted to look at. I wanted to see if I could not retrieve from the old images the person of my mother's stories, the girl full of flash and impudence. Sometimes I thought I could see her there, but mostly I could not. The girl in the pictures looked, as people had thought, shy. She was nobody I knew.

However she may have seemed to others, Ellen would always be interesting to my mother, because she was Ellen. To anyone else she had no distinction at all, save this one: that born into an Anglican family and married into a family that had its weddings and funerals in the United Church, Ellen had suddenly, at the age of 38, become a Catholic.

Nobody knew why, not even my mother. Nobody even knew how long she had been attending the Catholic Church.

"But she must have been going for quite a while, on the sly," Mrs. Wheeler said. "You don't just turn smack-bang like that, with no lead-up at all. I don't know if the Catholics would even have you that way."

Mrs. Wheeler had been angry, my mother said, when Willard and Ellen moved to Edmonton, and she was angry now. "It's Willard I feel sorry for," she said. "Thank heavens there are no children."

But if Willard Wheeler had any objections to make about his wife's conversion, nobody ever heard them. They said that he even went to the church when Ellen was baptized, or confirmed, or whatever it is that the Catholics do to you.

"I suppose she'll be after him to turn next," Mrs. Wheeler said. "You know what the Catholics are like."

All my mother could think of to say was that she was sure that Ellen had had her reasons, and that, knowing Ellen, the reasons would be good ones. But when Mrs. Wheeler had gone home, my mother let herself look as bewildered as she felt. "I wonder what ever came over Ellen," she said.

It was summertime and so Uncle Nathan, on holiday from teaching, was staying on the farm with us. "She hasn't said anything to you?" he asked.

My mother shook her head. "And I saw her three weeks ago when she must have known," she said.

We were silent for a minute. Then, "It isn't that I expect Ellen to tell me everything she does," my mother said. "Whatever Ellen does is all right with me." And then, with honesty, "It's just that I can't imagine what ever came over her."

Nor could she. The fact was that my mother, who could find stories in so many varieties of human experience, had little understanding of the religious impulse. She attended services at St. Chad's every second Sunday, which was as often as they were held, and liked the sense of community, of getting together with the same neighbours and relatives Sunday after Sunday for a lifetime, but she wasn't the type to understand mystical yearnings.

"Maybe she just felt the need for something in her life," Uncle Nathan said.

My mother looked bewildered. "She has Willard in her life," she said.

"So she has," Uncle Nathan said gently. "So she has."

My father, who was in the kitchen too, shifted in his chair, as if it had suddenly become uncomfortable. "I don't think we should talk about it," he said.

For once my mother agreed with him. "I don't have anything to say," she said.

I think that my mother thought that Ellen would discuss her conversion with her later, and then she would understand, and, if not be able to explain it to other people, at least have a story to tell herself about it. But Ellen said nothing, and it was Ellen's silence that Mother had to make a meaning out of.

"You grow up and you have your own lives," she said. "It's only natural."

But she felt left out. It was not, I knew, that my mother

felt that Ellen should have no secrets from her. She would never have expected Ellen to discuss her marriage with her, for instance, any more than she would have thought of discussing her own marriage with Ellen. But religion was different. Religion was a thing you practised in public. And if you thought you were on to a good thing, you ought to want to share it.

Other people were expecting Ellen to do that. They thought that Ellen, now that she was a Catholic, would try to convert them, and they discussed what they would say to her when she did. But Ellen said nothing about religion, to them or to my mother.

This made for certain difficulties. On a practical level, my mother found that Ellen's silence left her unarmed, unable to defend Ellen as well as she would have wished against Willard's mother. Mrs. Wheeler knew more about Ellen's religious comings and goings than my mother did, and the knowledge gave her the upper hand.

"They say she spends half her time dragging down to the church," Mrs. Wheeler said.

"You'd think she was some kind of servant," Mrs. Wheeler said.

"They say she's forever polishing pews and ironing altar cloths," Mrs. Wheeler said.

"She can't seem to get enough of it," Mrs. Wheeler said.

"Ellen was always a good-living person," my mother said. It was the best she could do.

I was twelve when Ellen converted, the age at which both religion and dramatic acts have their greatest appeal, and I found that Ellen's conversion made a great change in the picture of her I kept in my mind. By then I had just about lost faith in my mother's version of Ellen. Now Ellen, by her own act, had shown me a new reality, that there was much more to her than I had thought. And it seemed to me that I could understand the thing that had baffled my mother. My mother was different, too practical, too lacking in the inner life, to understand Ellen, who was another like me, I thought. Now when I thought of Ellen I thought neither of a tired-moving woman nor of a girl with tossing curls. I thought of a woman of serenity, of a face lit from within. Soon Ellen would come to visit us. I imagined the two of us alone. "I knew that *you* would understand, Maida," she would say. She would see in me a fellow seeker. "There are mysteries that are beyond our comprehension," she would say.

It occurred to me that I might myself become a Catholic. I might even become a nun. I took the white dresser scarf off my chest of drawers and stretched it across my forehead to see how I would look in a wimple. I imagined myself kneeling to receive (what *did* one receive when one became a nun?)... well, some kind of benediction...and I imagined Ellen standing behind me. She would be my godmother, I thought. (She already *was* my godmother, but I didn't think of that.) She would explain my decision to my parents, and I would explain hers.

Of course I was disappointed the first time Ellen came to the farm after her conversion. How could I have been otherwise? But after she had gone back home I began to wonder if maybe I had been mistaken. It seemed to me that the Ellen I had imagined was too real not to exist somewhere. Perhaps I would find her in her own house in the city, close to the place where she had had her religious thoughts.

I don't *think* I was expecting that Ellen's house would be changed. I know that Mrs. Wheeler was expecting *The Last Supper* in the dining-room and *The Sacred Heart* in the bedroom, but I don't think that I was. But I may have thought that there would be *something*. I had already noticed that people's houses were like phonograph records, that the things that happened in them were somehow recorded, that you could get funny feelings from the walls themselves.

Whatever I was expecting, when I next went to the city I found Ellen's house little changed from what it had always been. Her living-room furniture was still arranged around a plaster fireplace in which electric logs could be made to glow, but not give off heat. The only thing that was new was an ornament in the centre of the mantelpiece. It was a bowl of glass fruit with a light in the middle. When it was plugged in, grapes, cherries and plums glowed like bright, inedible jewels. It looked like something chosen by somebody else, Willard probably, as a gift. For that matter, everything in Ellen's house looked as if it might have been chosen by somebody else. There was no mark of her anywhere except, perhaps, in the room where she kept her sewing-machine and ironing-board. And Ellen's walls told me nothing. Either they were silent—things in the house were as they had always been—or else they spoke in some language inaudible to me.

I remember sitting with Ellen in the living-room that evening while Willard slept. Ellen was trying to knit a diamond sock. I say *was trying to knit*, because she wasn't having much luck at it. There were ten or twelve plastic bobbins suspended from the sock, designed to keep the different colours of wool from getting tangled up, but they hadn't served their function. Ellen turned the sock over and over in her hands, looking for a place to start disentangling the ganglia.

"It's too bad Mother isn't here to help you," I said, not thinking. My mother was considered to be clever with her hands.

Ellen smiled ruefully. "A woman my age ought to be able to untangle her own knitting," she said. What she meant was that to admit that this was so did not make it true. And then, "Your mother has been taking care of me all her life," she said. "When we were girls I used to follow her around like a puppy."

I thought only one word: *So.*

But after a minute I wasn't sure it was the right thing to

think. Ellen's version of their joint past didn't square with my mother's, but was one necessarily true and the other false?

It was as if Ellen knew what I was thinking. "I know a nun who speaks Spanish," she said. "And she says that one of the ways to say 'I remember' in Spanish is to say 'I make memory.' And that one of the ways to say 'I realize' is to say 'I give myself the story that...'"

I couldn't say anything. That was the closest, except for one other time, that Ellen and I ever came to each other, and I couldn't say anything. Not even what I thought, which was that there are languages truer than ours.

The reason I couldn't say anything was that Ellen had said *a nun*. She had said it as easily as you might say *a friend* or *an acquaintance*, but I hadn't heard it that way. What I had heard was a reference to her religion, and she had never made a reference to it before, and I wasn't prepared for it.

That was the last time I was ever in Ellen's house in Edmonton. Shortly afterwards Willard, who worked for the railway, bid on a job in the interior of BC and got it, and they moved away.

My mother was shocked and unhappy when she heard that they were going. Ellen's secrecy about her conversion had made her realize that their friendship was not as close as it had been, but Ellen was still *there*. Now she would not be. My mother grieved over Ellen's move as she might have over a final parting, and in a way, that was what it turned out to be. After they moved, Willard and Ellen came back every couple of years to visit Willard's mother, and then they would spend an afternoon or an evening with us. "Ellen and I always take up just where we left off," my mother would say, but it wasn't true. There was a distance between them now, an effort in the talking, and regret on both of their faces that this should be so.

When my mother didn't know what to talk about with

anyone, she told stories. One day when Ellen was visiting, she kept the conversation going by telling stories about me. "Have I ever told you about the time that Maida brought me a pailful of partridges?" she asked. And then she told the story. It was a story I told myself often.

Once, when I was still quite small, I was walking through the bush west of our house on a summer afternoon with a berry pail in my hand when I came upon a family of partridge chicks. They were tiny, just little balls of fluff, and they looked as insubstantial as puffs of breath on a winter morning. They looked as if they might vanish, dissolve, but they didn't. They stood there alive and blinking, astonished, as if they hadn't expected to see me either.

Ordinarily, partridges get away fast. You think you see them and then they are gone, and you are not sure whether there was anything there or not. But these chicks did not move. Maybe they were so tiny that they hadn't come into possession of their instincts yet. Life in the egg was standing still, and they hadn't had time to get used to any other kind. Or maybe a chick's instincts tell it to move only where its mother leads. Whatever the reason, these chicks stayed where they were, on the cow path at my feet.

They were small and perfect, exactly what they should have been. I felt as if I had been wanting this sight, had been needing it.

I bent down. At first it was enough just to look. But then I wanted to touch one with my finger. And then I wanted to hold it in the hollow of my hand. I sat for a while, crouched on the cow path, a chick in my hand, perfectly happy. Then I wanted to touch the chick with my face, to feel it against my cheek. I lifted it, and it smelled warm. It seemed to me that this was the most wonderful thing that had ever happened to me, that nothing could ever be more wonderful. But then it occurred to me that there was one more thing I needed to make what was happening perfect: I needed to share it with

115

somebody.

I put the chick into my berry pail. Then I picked up another one and put it in the pail too. It was like picking strawberries. When all the chicks were in the pail I got up and started for the house. I wanted to show them to my mother.

My mother was a good person to share things with. She took time to admire the chicks, to share my delight in them, before she told me that I would have to take them back. Their mother would be looking for them, she said. I should take them back to the place where I had found them.

I did that. And when I got to the place where I had found them I could hear their mother somewhere nearby, making throaty sounds, calling to them.

I wondered whether the chicks would go to her. Maybe they would feel, as I did, that they belonged with me. Maybe they would not want to leave me. I took a chick out of the berry pail and set it on the cow path.

It vanished. It didn't walk away or fly away, it simply disappeared. One minute there was a ball of fluff on the path, the next, nothing.

I set the chicks out one by one, and one by one they vanished. But one of them, as it stood on the path, said my name. *Maida.* It said it quite plainly in its little chick voice. Then it too was gone.

When my mother told Ellen about the partridges, as much about them as I had told her, I was surprised to see Ellen's eyes fill with tears. "It's not a thing you'd ever forget," she said, as if she knew that I thought of them often, that I felt as if I had received a command to be faithful to them. But then Ellen bent over and began to fuss with her stocking as if she didn't want me to see the tears in her eyes, and I stared at her, thinking that Ellen had at last become real to me. I had a sensation of speeding past my own past self, a self that had not quite realized that even tired people could be real.

The stories we tell, the stories we share. We tell them because we think there is an ear that will hear what we want to say, or we keep our stories quiet, for whatever reason. The next part of the story of Ellen was something I didn't hear until the summer I was seventeen, nearly as old as Ellen had been when it happened.

It was a hot July afternoon, the day that I heard it, and we were sitting in the kitchen having coffee. My father had been working in the fields and, although he had washed when he came in, his eyelashes were still sooty with summerfallow. It made him look more handsome than usual, and also more like Uncle Nathan, who was sitting beside him.

The kitchen smelled of peaches. My mother had bought two cases and they had all ripened at once, and she was canning them.

How did we happen to be talking about Ellen? I don't know. I only know that Uncle Nathan said how pretty Ellen had been when she was a girl and that my mother agreed. "I have a picture of her with her saddle pony in which she is positively radiant," she said.

I thought that I knew all of my mother's pictures, but I could remember no picture of Ellen with a pony. When I said so, my mother hesitated a second. "It's one of a bunch of snapshots I keep in my dresser drawer," she said finally. She told me that I could get them out, and I did. But when I had spread them on the kitchen table I saw that most of the pictures were not of Ellen, but of a young man, a boy who did not look like any of the families in our district. When I had found the pictures of Ellen and her pony—there were several —I realized that I was at last seeing the Ellen that my mother wanted me to see. The Ellen in these pictures had a sort of bloom on her; she looked like a girl on the brink of something marvellous. She faced the camera laughing, and there was a confidence about her that was almost triumph. Why, I wondered, had I never seen these pictures before?

My mother took a minute to answer. Then, "Those pictures were taken by Danny Malone," she said. "If Ellen had ever seen them, she would have remembered that."

It did not take much perception to figure out that the young man in the other pictures, the handsome boy with the laughing eyes, must be Danny Malone. He even *looked* as if his name would be Danny Malone. But why had I never heard of him until now?

"I suppose I should have told you about Danny," my mother said. "I really should have told you." She meant that parents had an obligation to tell their children about life, and that Danny Malone had been part of the life she had known, and that his story might contain something that I would need to know to live mine.

"It was something over and done with," my father said.

Whatever the reason for my mother's silence, I knew that this was not it. "It was just that Danny and Ellen almost got married," she said. "It doesn't seem right to talk about people who don't get married to each other."

I knew what she meant. In Willow Bunch, when people married other people, they belonged to *those* people. You didn't talk about the people they might have married, at least not if they were people you cared about.

But I could see that my mother was asking herself what harm it would do now, and my father could see her thinking it too. "Now you don't want to go dragging all that old stuff up," he said.

"It was a long time ago," my mother said.

But she still seemed undecided. Finally, "Danny Malone was a boy from Prince Edward Island," she said to me. "He came out to help with the harvest the fall that Ellen and I were eighteen, and he stayed until after the harvest the next year. He and Ellen were engaged for a while."

I knew from my mother's other stories that engaged did not always mean married, and that there was usually more story when it didn't. But my mother began to peel peaches as if that was all she meant to say.

I spread the pictures on the table in front of me, to see what meaning I could get from *them*. I saw Danny Malone leaning against a loaded hayrack in one picture, Danny Malone holding the bridle of Ellen's saddle pony in another. There was a look of vitality about him; he looked like a boy ready to take on the world. In another picture, a picture that looked like it might have been taken when Danny didn't know there was anyone there, he was lying on the grass and reading a book, and I thought that I had never before noticed what an attractive activity book-reading is in a man. There were several pictures of Danny and Ellen together. In one he had his arm around her, and she had his hat on her head, and both of them were laughing.

Uncle Nathan moved his chair so that he could see the pictures too. "I heard that Danny did pretty well for himself after he left Willow Bunch," he said finally.

"So they said," my mother said. "It runs in my mind that he owned a fleet of 40 trucks at the time he died." And then, "It's been eight years," she said. "Just think. Eight years."

"Danny always did have a lot of ambition," Uncle Nathan said. He was using *ambition* in the local sense, meaning energy, get-up-and-go. "There was never any dust on Danny Malone."

My mother finished filling one quart sealer and began to slice peaches into another. "They used to say he could stook all day and dance all night," she said. "And my, couldn't he dance?"

"I remember seeing Danny and Ellen together at a dance once," Uncle Nathan said. "It was in lilac time."

I relaxed then. With both Uncle Nathan and my mother remembering, the story would come.

"If I could have just one wish, it would be to dance the old time waltz with Danny Malone just one more time before I died," my mother said.

I was used to my mother's hyperbole. She loved to dance, and she remembered all her old dancing partners with fondness, all the wonderful waltzers and square-dancers and seven-steppers who had danced with her and then moved away. To my mother, living without dancing was no living at all.

Unfortunately, my father was an indifferent dancer. When we went to dances he would trundle my mother around the floor once, to give other men permission to dance with her, and then he would retire to a masculine corner to talk seed drills and combines. My mother would go on dancing, and she never lacked for partners.

When he was staying with us, Uncle Nathan was one of them. Uncle Nathan was an inspired dancer, and he danced best of all when he danced with my mother. Seeing them together, you would feel that no music was complete until they had taken ahold of it and sung it out through their bodies. The music would stop and they would stop dancing, and their faces would slowly return to the room they were in. Then Uncle Nathan would thank Mother for the dance and walk her back to the benches where the ladies sat, and then both of them would dance with other people.

My mother finished the last sealer and stood up to pour sugar syrup over her peaches. Then she set the lids and rubber rings in place, and put the sealers in the canner. After that she washed her hands and came over to look at the pictures.

"You can see how good-looking Ellen was then," she said to me. "And coming into the district from outside, Danny saw right away what the local boys had been too blind to see."

Had Danny been her first boyfriend then?

"First and only," my mother said. "Other than Willard, of course."

"Now that's enough of that," my father said.

But my mother had had time to think it over, and she had

made a decision, and she went on talking to show us what it was.

"I was the one who brought Danny and Ellen together," she said, and she spoke as proudly as if Danny and Ellen had gone on to celebrate their twenty-fifth wedding anniversary. "There was a boy who was turning up at our place on Sundays —he was sweet on *me*—and I got him to bring Danny with him, and I saw to it that Ellen was there."

Danny and Ellen took to each other right away, my mother said. "In those days we didn't exactly go around two-by-two the way young people do now. We all went everyplace in a group. But Danny and Ellen paired off right away."

She hesitated then, as if her story had brought her to a word she was shy of using, but she used it anyway. "Danny and Ellen were very much in love," she said.

My father was silent. I think he knew that when my mother had gone this far, there wasn't a chance that she wouldn't go on. And Uncle Nathan was a storyteller too. "That dance I saw them at," he said. "In lilac time. Do you remember it?"

My mother nodded, and a faraway expression came onto her face and she began to tell the story.

It was in the spring of the year, and my mother and Ellen were nineteen. A group of young people had gone to the dance together, and my mother remembered it all. She remembered driving into town while it was still daylight. She remembered the look of the fields, the crops coming up, the black dirt still visible between the rows of emerging grain. She remembered that it was too early in the year to tell the wheat from the oats or the barley. She remembered the grass in the ditches, red-topped and surprisingly tall. She remembered the buffalo beans in bloom, and the stiff white yarrow, golden in the long light of evening. And she remembered the shadow of the car they were riding in, square-topped and tall in the evening light, racing along the road allowance beside them. Sometimes they would slow for a bend in the road and then the scent of the evening would catch at them through the open windows. And she remembered Danny Malone's voice saying, "It's a night out of heaven, Ellen. A night out of heaven."

"I think of Danny and Ellen every year when the lilacs are in bloom," my mother said.

"So do I," Uncle Nathan said. "And once a year it's lilac time."

When they got to town, the whole town smelled of lilacs, my mother said. There were lilacs blooming everywhere.

Uncle Nathan and my mother began now to share the telling of the story. They remembered the dance, and the supper waltz, and that Danny and Ellen had gone for a walk during the break for midnight lunch. They remembered that Danny had begun to pick lilacs, a bough from every bush they passed, and had given the lilacs to Ellen. When the time came to go back to the dance, Ellen couldn't bear to throw her bouquet away.

"And so she brought them in and she and Danny danced the first dance with Ellen holding the lilacs," my mother said.

"She had them in her hand, over Danny's shoulder," Uncle Nathan said. "She looked just like a bride."

"People stopped dancing and formed a circle around them and Danny and Ellen danced in the middle, just as if it was their wedding dance," my mother said.

We were all quiet then for a while, thinking of that night in springtime so long ago. Then, "Danny used to say 'She's a gift from heaven'" my mother said.

It would have been nice if the story could have stopped there, with a marriage implied, a happy ending hoped for. But it hadn't turned out that way, and I wanted to know why.

My mother went back to peeling peaches. "Danny was a Catholic," she said in reply to my question. Her hands were working quickly now. "At first it didn't occur to either of

them that the difference in religion would make any difference." But then...well, my mother, who wished it had happened otherwise, had been there on the day that they broke
up.

It was a Sunday in autumn, and Ellen and Danny had gone
horseback-riding, taking my mother with them. Ellen had
packed a lunch, and they stopped on a hillface overlooking
the river to eat it. It was quiet, sitting there in the thin
sunshine of late October, looking out over bluffs bare of leaves
except for the crown of new growth at the top. A wasp's nest,
vacant now, hung in a hollow stump near where they were
sitting on the brown grass. Seeing it there made her realize,
my mother said, how quiet everything was. There was no
sound of bees. No sound of birds either. The robins and the
meadowlarks and the killdeer had all gone south. The leaves
were gone and the bees were gone and the birds were gone,
but there was a feeling of rightness about the day, my mother
said, of things happening in their season. What else should
you be listening to on an October day but the sound of dry
grass rustling, of saddle ponies grazing?

The conversation was lazy. Danny and Ellen were talking
about being married to each other, were making jokes about
it, kidding one another about who would have to get up in
the morning to light the fire, about who would cut the
kindling. And then talk turned to their wedding, and Danny
said something about the church, and it was evident, my
mother said, that he saw the wedding as happening in a
Catholic church.

"Of course you'll have to be received into the Church first,"
he said. "That is, if they'll have you."

His voice was easy. It was more of the same kind of talk
they had been making, but it was clear, my mother said, that
he was taking Ellen's conversion for granted, that no other
possibility had ever crossed his mind.

Ellen's family, the Lockerbies, were Anglican, as we were,

but none of us were *very* Anglican, and my mother had never supposed that religion meant very much to Ellen one way or the other. And so she was not surprised when Ellen answered, her voice as easy as Danny's had been. "And what makes you think I should be the one to turn?"

Danny reached over and rumpled her hair. "Silly, silly girl," he said. "Of course you'd have to change."

My mother said she didn't know what happened then... inside of Ellen, that is. Telling us about it, she listed the possibilities. It might have been, she said, that Ellen minded Danny taking her conversion for granted that way. It might have been that Ellen cared more about her own religion than anybody had thought. Or it might have been that she was testing her power over Danny, proving to herself that he must love her a lot, since he put up with so much nonsense from her. Whatever Ellen was thinking, her voice took on an almost quarrelsome note. "Just don't be too sure of me, Danny," she said.

Danny was reaching forward to stuff a crumpled sandwich paper into an empty lunch bag. His head gave a little jerk of surprise. Then he looked at Ellen. And when he spoke again there was no joking in him.

"You'd have to change, Ellen," he said. "You'd be the mother of my children."

My mother said that she had wished ever since that she had got on her horse right then and ridden away from that hillside. "Left by themselves they might have worked things out," she said. "If they had been alone, they would have touched each other. And then it would have been all right."

My father shifted in his chair, but he said nothing.

My mother went on. At that time, to ride away seemed impossible, she said. It would have seemed too conspicuous, like a confirmation of what had to be denied, that what was happening was serious.

"They'd be my children too, you know," Ellen said. Her

voice was high and thin, the way it is when you've had the wind knocked out of you, and there was an ugly red flush on her face. "If you think all you have to do is whistle and I'll give up my religion, you've got another think coming."

"Ellen, Ellen," Danny said, and the alarm in his voice was close to despair. He bent his head for a moment, and pulled a handful of dry grass out of the hillside and held it in his hand. "If you wouldn't convert... if you really felt you couldn't do it ..." His voice trailed off. But after a moment he gathered himself together and finished what he had to say. "If you felt you couldn't convert, then I don't see how we could be married," he said.

My mother said that Ellen did not blink an eye. "Then I guess we'd better not get married," she said.

Danny's lips were white. "I never realized, Ellen," he whispered. "I never realized."

"I don't think it ever occurred to Ellen that Danny would accept what she had said as her final word in the matter," my mother said.

"You wouldn't think he *would* have," Uncle Nathan said.

"It was different with Danny," my mother said. "You've got to remember he would never have changed himself. I suppose he thought that Ellen felt the same way about it."

My mother got up to check her peaches. She lifted the canner lid and a cloud of steam came out. Then she lifted the rack of sealers and carried it to an old washstand to cool, out of the draft.

"Do you think Ellen *would* have changed?" Uncle Nathan asked.

"In a minute," my mother said.

"Then why...?"

"I don't think Ellen liked Danny putting conditions on it like that," she said. "No girl would. She wanted Danny to want her even if she was a Protestant."

There was a look of wonder on Uncle Nathan's face at the

ways of women and girls. "You don't mean to tell me that Ellen sent Danny away because he hadn't said the thing right?" he asked.

"Well, I think she planned to give in later," my mother said. "But the next time Danny came, it was to say goodbye."

We were all quiet then. There was a feeling in the room of a story unfinished, a summing up needed. After a minute, Uncle Nathan attempted to provide it. "I suppose what happened then may have had something to do with Ellen turning Catholic all those years later," he said.

I had been thinking the same thing, but my mother looked upset when he said it. "I wouldn't want to think that," she said. And then, "I can't see any connection. No connection at all."

A series of complicated expressions crossed Uncle Nathan's face. He spoke hurriedly. "Probably you're right," he said. "Probably there was no connection."

But my mother still looked troubled. "Danny was one part of Ellen's life and Willard was another," she said. "And Ellen turned Catholic in Willard's part."

"That's right too," Uncle Nathan said.

My father stirred in his chair. "It was all a long, long time ago," he said.

I had been looking at my mother and Uncle Nathan, first at one and then at the other, but now I looked at my father. I saw that he looked relaxed now, even expansive. The story was over and the time of uneasiness had passed.

"Danny and Ellen were sweet on each other for a while, but that's over and done with," he said, his voice dismissing all probing into the past as a thing that got you nowhere. He spoke as if *he* would give them the meaning to their story. "It's over and done with," he said again. "And there's been a lot of water flow under the bridge since then."

THRESHING TIME

There were three people in the room, counting the child. The house they were sitting in belonged to the smaller man, but a stranger coming into the room might have thought otherwise. The small man, whose name was Black, was seated in a rocking-chair, but he was not rocking. Instead, he was leaning forward, so far forward that only the front arc of his rockers made contact with the floor. He looked as if he might be waiting for some sign—to speak, perhaps, or to jump to his feet to perform some task.

It was the big man, the older man, who was at his ease. His name was Max Staunton. He sat on the Winnipeg couch, leaning back, his eyes surveying the room. There was not very much in it to look at, but what there was his eyes took in. They took in the printed curtain hanging across the doorway to the front bedroom. They took in the sewing-machine treated as a table, with a cloth on top. They took in the unlighted lamp and its clean chimney. When they came to the corner of the room, they took in the radio. It was a small one and it sat on a cloth-skirted box. Its striped batteries were on the floor beneath, but the wires that should have connected radio and batteries to outdoor aerial had been yanked from the wall; they curled crazily in the air.

Staunton's eyes stopped and considered the wires. Finally, "Radio not working?" he asked.

Black looked embarrassed.

"It works if it's connected," he said.

The third person in the room, the child, was seated on Staunton's lap, but her body wasn't adjusted for lap-sitting. She held herself stiffly, as carefully as if she were perched on a high rail fence. Staunton was a stranger to father and daughter alike, but the daughter was at an additional disadvantage: she could not see the man. All she knew of him was what she could tell by feel. That and what she had seen when he arrived a few minutes before.

Black had been sitting on the back porch mending harness when Staunton's car drove into the yard. The child was beside him. They looked up and where a moment before there had been only pin-cherry bushes and the dooryard gate, there now was a man. He was big: tall and powerfully built, but big-bellied with middle age.

Staunton saw them at the same time as they saw him, and when he saw them, he stopped. He hooked his thumbs through the belt of his trousers and smiled. He had an unusual way of smiling. His bottom lip came out when he did it.

"I'm looking for a fellow by the name of Owen Black," he said.

Owen stood up. "You just found him," he said.

They shook hands then, and went into the house, the child following them. Staunton was at his ease from the very first, his eyes looking around freely. He might have been trying to assure Owen that he had been coming into such places all his life.

Staunton had lifted the child onto his lap when he sat down and she remained where he had put her, waiting to find out what was expected of her.

"This is a fine little girl you've got here," Staunton said. His voice was a gentle boom. It was a voice that was at a variance with his appearance, but Owen didn't notice that. He didn't meet many strangers; he didn't get much practice in assessing them.

"Your daddy's a lucky man to have a nice little girl like you," Staunton said to the child, whose name was Estelle.

"I don't have any little people at my house." He tilted his head back and his bottom lip came out as he smiled. "My little boy got to be big a long time ago," he said.

Something about the way he spoke suggested that Max Staunton was performing for an invisible audience. It was as if there was another Max Staunton standing by watching, a man whose approval he counted on.

The child did not move. There was an awareness of strangeness in her face. There was strange flesh—strange thigh, strange arm—brought into contact, almost into contact, with her own flesh. She hadn't been able to decide how to feel about it.

She was wearing a thin cotton dress with a sash at the waist. Her arms and legs were bare. She wore canvas shoes, darned at the toes, but no stockings. Her feet and legs protruded awkwardly, in the position they had taken when Staunton put her where she was. She made no attempt to move. It was as if to her mind, to slide away, to reclaim possession of her own body, was an act somehow related to disobedience. A thought not thinkable.

At ordinary times Owen took pride in his daughter's silence, her compliance with visitors, but at the moment he wasn't thinking about her at all. He was thinking about Staunton. He had heard of Staunton before, but this was the first time he had seen him. It seemed to Owen that the man was different from what he would have expected.

In what way, different? Owen couldn't say. Confronted with the reality, Owen couldn't remember what it was that he had been expecting. Or say how Staunton differed from it. Owen's thoughts didn't come to him in words.

From the kitchen there came the sound of a stove lid being lifted and replaced, and then the clink of water dipper against tea kettle. If Owen had been asked what the sounds meant, he could have told you that Josie was in the kitchen making coffee. But he wasn't asked, and his mind didn't comment.

"I suppose you've heard that I'm in the market for men," Staunton said then.

Owen nodded. He had heard that. He supposed that was why Staunton was here: to give him a job.

"Not that I expect to have any trouble making up a crew," Staunton said. "There are men growing on the trees this fall." Staunton's hand was toying with a curl of cotton stuffing that had pushed its way through the worn covering of the Winnipeg couch. "Most of the outfits are filled up," he said. "But I can still take on one more team."

Owen leaned back then, waiting, and the middle of his rockers made contact with the floorboards. But instead of offering Owen the job, Staunton began to talk about who he would be threshing. "We start at the Allsopps' tomorrow," he said. "And then we'll do the Larsons. And after that, the Beckers."

He had taken out tobacco and papers and was rolling a cigarette, his arm still around the child. He stopped speaking to lick the paper. "You'll come after the Beckers," he told Owen. "That is, *if* I'm doing you."

Owen leaned forward again. He didn't understand what Staunton was telling him. Of course Staunton would be threshing him...unless he wasn't working for Staunton. Was Staunton trying to tell him that he might not get the job?

Owen wished that he knew more about Max Staunton. He knew that Staunton had bought the Hubble place south of town last fall, and that he had moved up after the crops were off. Staunton had come from farther south in the province. Owen knew that Staunton had a threshing-machine and that he had a grown son, a boy with an unusual name. The reason Staunton was threshing north of town instead of in his own district was that the north country was short of threshing outfits and the south wasn't. Owen knew that much about him.

Now it seemed that Staunton wanted to add to his knowledge. "I've taken off a lot of crops in my day," Staunton was saying. He hooked his thumbs through his belt and smiled. "If I don't know what I'm doing by now, I guess I never will," he said.

He stopped then, as if he expected that Owen would want to say something. He was smiling, he seemed friendly. But when Owen remained silent, a look that resembled displeasure came on to his face. It was only there for a moment. Then Staunton sort of took it off and put it away, as if in storage.

After a minute, "Anyway, it's Elreno who runs the outfit now," Staunton said pleasantly. "His old dad is just the flunky."

Elreno was the name of Staunton's son. Owen had heard that Elreno was his father's tractor man. Staunton himself looked after the separator. But as to who was boss...well, Owen had taken it for granted that Staunton would be.

"Elreno's a good man," Staunton was saying. He smiled again. "You know how it will take some men half the night to line up an outfit?" he said. "Well, Elreno gets it right first try, every time. And he's never had a belt slide off yet."

Owen tried to think of something to say. The room they were sitting in was warm. Josie had washed the wooden floor earlier to cool the house off, but the heat was starting to come back.

"I don't say this because he's my son," Staunton went on, "but I can tell you that Elreno is going to be a good man at handling men too." He shifted the child from right knee to left. "That was something I taught him myself," he said. And then, as if to explain, "There are some men that would walk all over you if you didn't stand up for your rights," Staunton said.

When he had said that, he stopped again. Again it was as if he thought that Owen would want to say something, but again Owen was silent. And again the look of displeasure crossed Staunton's face.

Owen didn't see it. He was watching Staunton and listening to him, but he wasn't taking in what Staunton was telling him with either his voice or his face. *Offer me a job,* he was thinking. *Offer me a job.*

He had to have a job. Otherwise...

There was no otherwise. It had come to this: Estelle had no shoes but the canvas ones she had on her feet, and they had darns in the toes. It had come to this: he and Josie had only one set of winter chore clothes between them; if they had a two-man job to do, they had to wait for a warm day to do it. Josie was making her slips and underdrawers out of flour sacks. Owen couldn't bear to think about them; he turned over in bed and faced the wall every night when she undressed. It had come to this: they owed money for seed and twine and groceries. They did without whatever they could. Some things, like a radio licence, they never even considered buying. Josie had to scramble like a thief to disconnect the radio whenever a strange car slowed down on the road. But there were things they couldn't do without: flour, coal oil, felt socks.

Relief? It was out of the question. Josie's father didn't believe in it. "Any man who can't feed his own family is a pretty poor excuse for a man," he said, and Owen agreed with him. As far as he knew, so did Josie.

But it wasn't easy, staying off relief. There were times when Owen thought that he had reached the breaking point. But he had always hung on somehow. He had felt as if he was going to break down so many times that he no longer took the feeling seriously. He knew that some people really did have breakdowns, but he also knew that he wasn't one of them. He hung on. Only he got so tired.

Owen could remember what it had felt like to enjoy his body, to rejoice in its energies. But now, coming in from the field or from choring, "I'm no good for anything anymore," he would think. Only it wasn't just working that made him tired. He could be tired even after a rainy day. He was so tired all the time that he never really felt like doing anything. He was too tired even for Josie.

Sometimes Josie would be helping him with a job, or he would be helping her. They could be doing anything: digging potatoes, mending binder canvas, banking up the house for winter...and it would come into Owen's head that Josie was thinking about *that*. Then he would have to look away. Because there was nothing he could do to help it.

Once, when he would be doing other things, going about his work, he used to find himself thinking about Josie, and what they did together, and the thinking gave him pleasure. He hadn't known then that it would come to an end so soon, before either of them was 30. Nobody had told him that that happened. Somebody should have, he thought. If they had, he would have made hay while the sun shone, so to speak. He wouldn't have wasted a single opportunity.

Now, since there was nothing to be done about it, he preferred not to think about it at all. He put it out of his mind. If he wanted something nice to think about, he thought about Estelle.

It seemed to Owen that the feelings he had about Estelle were not dependent upon her being his daughter. He believed that even if she had belonged to somebody else, he still would have been able to perceive her essential quality, which was purity. He didn't use that word to describe her, and it was only part of what he meant when he said, "She's just pure Estelle." The other part was that there was nothing "put on" about Estelle. She was the same thing from pith to peel. Compared to her, other children seemed to Owen to be artificial and calculating. It seemed to him that they treated themselves not as people but as things: things that they used to produce effects, to gain attention. Owen was glad that Estelle wasn't like that.

Sitting on Staunton's lap now, Estelle was less stiff than she had been, but her eyes were still questioning, unsure. Staunton seemed to be trying to get her to relax. He had her hand in his, and her arm on his, and he was bouncing their two arms up and down together. There was a cadence to the motion, as when a man dandles a baby on his foot, or taps his toe to music. But he was fondling Estelle without really giving her his attention. His attention was on Owen.

"You know," Staunton said, "there are men around this fall who want a job so bad they'd crawl to get it." He shook his head, as if inviting Owen to share his wonder at how bad things had got to be. Then, "They told me you were wanting a job," he said.

Owen eased back on his rockers. "They told you right," he said.

Staunton nodded. "There have been a lot of men after me for jobs," he said.

Owen felt the need to speak up on his own behalf. "Those would be men without teams," he said. He wanted to see things settled. He wanted to remind Staunton that he had a team.

But Staunton looked displeased. "Men with teams and men without," he said shortly.

Staunton had given up bouncing the child's arm. Now the fingers of his right hand were pulling a piece of stuffing out of the couch. His left hand was cupped over Estelle's knee, and one finger was moving back and forth, back and forth, tracing an arc on the soft skin on the inside of her knee. Both hands busy, but his eyes someplace else. His eyes were on Owen's face.

Estelle's eyes, too, sought her father's.

"It makes it hard for me," Staunton said. "I can't say yes to one without saying no to another."

Owen looked out the window. His eyes came to rest on the pin-cherry bushes. What was it that Staunton wanted him to say? *Whatever deal you're offering, it's all right with me?* That would be the truth, but it wasn't a thing that Owen cared to hear said in words.

"You'd be surprised at how desperate some people are getting," Staunton said.

Josie came in then with the coffee things, and when she had brought them everything they needed, left them alone again.

Then Staunton began to play a tickling game with the child.

"The little wood tick went *here*," he said, and his fingers walked in tiny, tiny footsteps up from her wrist..."and *here* ..." they reached the inside of her elbow. "And *here*!" They invaded the hollow place underneath her arm.

The child collapsed in Staunton's arms, wriggling with pleasure.

Owen shuddered. He wanted to say *You cut that out.* He

135

played tickling games with Estelle himself, but it seemed to him that Staunton's game was different from his game. In his game it was *the little mousie* who crawled up arms. There might have been another difference too, but Owen couldn't put a name to what it was. In any case, the difference between wood ticks and mousies was enough.

As far as he knew, Owen had never seen a wood tick, but as a boy he had been told about them. He had been told that a wood tick could bite you and you wouldn't even feel it. But if you didn't see the wood tick on your skin and get him off by lighting a match and holding it to him, he would eat his way inside of you. And if he got inside, it would be too late. He would eat his way up your bloodstream and when he got to your heart you would die.

Owen was disgusted with himself when he realized that he, a grown man, had been about to speak out over a thing that was silly: the kind of thing that boys invent to scare each other with. Owen didn't even know if such a creature as a wood tick really existed. Even so, he wished that Staunton would stop playing with Estelle. Owen wanted to talk business. Staunton had obviously come to offer him a job. He hadn't come here for any other purpose. What, then, was holding him back?

As soon as Owen put the question to himself, an answer occurred. It could be because of his size.

Owen Black was a small man, as he had been a small boy. As a boy, he had learned that survival depended on staying out of fights. As a man, he was learning that it depended on doing more than you had it in you to do. Keeping on: that was what counted. And Staunton might not know it, but Owen could do that. Tired or not, he could keep on going. He had never stopped yet.

Last year had been a killer, but it hadn't killed him. Neither had the year before. He had thought it was going to. In the beginning there was only the dust and the chaff and the itching under your underwear. Later there was the exhaustion. And then the working beyond exhaustion. Sometimes, at the very last, the exhaustion would leave him. At those times Owen seemed to himself to leave his body, to be standing outside of it, not feeling anything. It was as if he were hovering in the air above and looking down at his own body. It seemed very small and far away. But it was still doing its work, still obeying orders.

There was nothing that Staunton could dish out that he couldn't take. Owen wanted to tell him that. He leaned forward, willing Staunton to offer him a job. He wanted to hear it put into words, to know that things were settled.

You want to work for me? Yes, I do. No more than that was needed. There was no need to talk about pay. Staunton would pay what all the outfits were paying this year: $1.50 a day for a man; $2.50 for a man with a team.

Staunton stopped playing with Estelle. Suddenly, "Do you break your own horses?" he asked.

Owen shook his head. He was considered a good man with horses, but he couldn't break them.

"I used to break horses," Staunton said. "When I was younger, I used to be able to swing a line and raise a blister under a horse's coat. I had enough strength in my shoulders for that." He smiled, remembering. "We used to practise," he said. "Some of us young fellows. We'd set up some bottles and then we'd swing our lines at them till we broke them."

He spoke as a man discussing his craft. "If you want to break horses for threshing, you've got to be able to lace them within an inch of their lives," he said. "The only way you can get an unbroke team to go up to the machinery is to make them scareder of what's behind them than what's in front of them."

Owen nodded. He knew that what Staunton said was true, but he couldn't do it himself. He had got Frank Deacon to break his horses for threshing.

"I'm not too happy about the team I'm putting into the field this year," Staunton went on. "They've threshed before. But I wouldn't say they were broke. A team's not broke until you can trust them."

Owen was impatient. It was jobs, not horse-breaking, that he wanted to hear talked about. But then Staunton began to do that. Sort of. At least he edged into the topic sideways. He told Owen that he docked his men for moving time. He considered himself a pretty good man to work for, he said, but he had never been able to see why a man should expect to be paid for time when he wasn't doing a blessed thing.

Owen kept his silence. If you didn't agree with a man, there wasn't much you could say to him. He could have told Staunton that people around here didn't think much of a man who docked his men 20¢ every time he moved the separator from one field to another. He felt as if he ought to tell him that, for his own good.

But before Owen could make up his mind to speak, Staunton had begun to talk about working hours. "Most of the outfits around here are in the field from 6 to 7," he said. "Well, so am I. But I'm not going to shut down at 7 if another hour will get a field finished."

Suddenly Staunton smiled. He looked like a man who has just thought of a good story.

"A kind of funny thing happened on my outfit last year," he said. "There was a guy working for me by the name of Jake Inkom. The men called him Inky. And Inky was a good worker, I'll say that for him. But he was a born troublemaker. Well, I could see that he was getting to be too big for his britches, that I was going to have to take him down a peg or two. But before I could get around to doing anything about it, he came up to me one day.

"I remember the way he looked when he come up," Staunton said. "There was a wind blowing over the summerfallow across the road from the place where we were picking up, and he was black as a nigger. He looked kind of like a nigger anyway. At least to me he did. And he stood there, with his ears full of the neighbour's summerfallow, and he wanted to know what time I was figuring on quitting that night. The men were getting fed up with working late every night, he said.

"'Oh,' I said. 'This is the first I've heard of it. Nobody's mentioned it to me.'

"'Well they are,' he said.

"'Oh, I don't like to hear that,' I said. 'I don't like having men on my outfit who aren't happy.'"

To Owen, "I just let him think that over for a minute," Staunton said. "And then I said, 'I'll tell you another thing I don't like, Inky,' I said. 'I don't like a man who thinks he knows more than I do about how I ought to run my outfit.' I said it loud, so that the other men could hear it. 'If there's any men here who don't like the time I start and the time I stop, I'd appreciate it if they'd say so right now,' I said. 'Because I can find someone to take their place without any trouble at all. And I wouldn't want anybody who wasn't happy working for me.'

"Inky dropped his head then, and I could see his jawbones grinding. But Inky wasn't a fool. After a minute he went back about his business.

"And you know," Staunton finished, smiling, "I never had no more trouble with him after that."

Owen tried to push his mind around the story Staunton had told him, but it wouldn't go there. He felt tired, as if there was some force pulling at him from inside, drawing him together and making him smaller.

"I think I'm a pretty easy man to get along with," Staunton said. He smiled then, that odd smile with the bottom lip pushed out. "Mind you," he said, "if a man's looking for trouble, I don't mind seeing to it that he gets it."

There was nothing for Owen to say. Nothing in his experience had prepared him to deal with a man like Staunton.

Staunton fixed Owen with his eyes. "I like a man to know what he's getting into when I hire him," he said. "That way, I don't have to listen to any bellyaching later."

Owen looked away. His eyes came to rest on the disconnected wires of the radio, curling crazily in the air. He felt that he had to speak. "I've never had any trouble on any of the outfits I've worked for," he said.

But then he found that he didn't like the sound of what he had said.

"Mind you, I guess I can bellyache as good as the next one," he added.

A hard look came into Staunton's eyes. He turned his attention away from Owen, toward the child. The palm of his hand was on her chest, curved over the place where one day she would have breasts. There were two pockets on the bodice of her dress, one over each breast. With the forefinger of his right hand, Staunton began to trace the outline made by rickrack braid around the right pocket.

The child's face took on a secretive look. It was as if she knew something, but for reasons of her own was pretending not to. She sat very still, one end of her sash between her fingers.

Again Owen felt his lack of experience with strangers. He could see that Estelle had lost her fear of Staunton. Her lips were parted and her eyes were half-closed. It was as if her attention was turned inward.

Staunton shifted Estelle's body from his right knee to his left, and then his left forefinger began to circle, following the outline of her pocket. The little nipples were visible, stiff as shoe buttons, through the cotton of her dress.

"*Estelle!*"

Owen's voice came out sharp. He startled himself and the child.

He made himself speak in a more normal voice. "You run

along now," he said. "You've been pestering Mr. Staunton long enough."

But Staunton's hand stayed on Estelle's chest, holding her. "She's no bother," he said. "Let her stay where she is."

It seemed to Owen that there was nothing he could say. All grownups played with children. If there was something different about the way Staunton did it, Owen didn't have a name for what the difference was. Maybe there was no difference. Maybe it was all in his head.

Staunton's finger had gone back to its gentle circling, but his attention wasn't on the child now. It was as if she—as if *Estelle*—did not exist for him. There was something on his lap and he was fondling it. But his eyes were on Owen. It was Owen he was getting his pleasure from.

Again Owen felt that force inside of him, pulling him into a smaller knot. What was a man supposed to do? But when he asked himself that question, his thoughts turned aside, retreated. He lowered his eyes before Staunton's steady gaze. They came to rest on Estelle's feet: her canvas shoes, the darned toes of them. He did not speak.

After a moment it seemed to him that Staunton had known he would not speak. Owen stirred then and his rocking-chair creaked. The room had got hotter. He was sweating. He felt as if his body was telling him something. He became aware of hands clutched on the arms of his chair, of toes arched, pressed so hard against the soles of his boots that they ached. His neck felt weak, unable to hold up his head. And then his stomach cramped sharply and he realized that if he didn't get up and walk away from here, he was going to be sick.

He stood up. "I better get back to my harness," he said.

Staunton stood up too. "Not so fast," he said.

He spoke like a man who liked to do the leaving; a man who wouldn't be left. "You haven't told me yet whether you want to work for me or not."

Owen knew what he ought to say. He ought to say *I can*

stand it if you can. Something that, by making a joke of it, would make it sound like he had a choice. But he didn't risk it.

"I do," he said.

"All right then," Staunton said. "Be at the Allsopps' for breakfast tomorrow morning."

Then he turned to go. He was the first one out of the house.

On the path, Estelle caught up with Staunton and reached up to take his hand. And then, when Staunton looked down, the child simpered up at him. *She's making eyes,* Owen thought.

Owen followed Staunton and Estelle out to the gate, keeping his eyes fastened on the pin-cherry bushes. Their leaves were red. He did not look at the child, who was prancing, her body motions jerky, showing off.

Owen had no name for the way he was feeling but he did know that there was something that he should have done, and that he hadn't done it. But when should he have done it? When did it stop being too soon and start being too late?

When they got to the gate, Staunton put his hand into his pocket and pulled out a quarter. He gave it to Estelle. He did it carelessly, to show how little a quarter meant to him.

Owen broke a branch off the pin-cherry bush and began to strip off its leaves. They fell from his fingers, red as blood. Then Staunton got into his car, backed it out and was gone.

Owen turned to go back to the house.

Then, "Daddy," Estelle said. There was a sound in her voice that had never been there before. It was whining, self-important.

When Owen turned to look at her, she tilted her head back and hooked her thumbs into the sash at her waist. Her lower lip came out as she smiled.

"Daddy," Estelle said. "I want..."

She didn't get any further. Owen seized her by the arm, stopping speech.

"You try a trick like that again and I'll tan you good," he said.

Then he dropped her arm. It was as if he could not bear to touch her flesh with his. He turned his back on her and walked toward the house. But when he got to the back step, he turned again to look at her. The child stood where he had left her. An expression, and then an expression, and then another passed across her face. The consciousness of her own importance had left her now, and she seemed curiously unprotected without it.

She stood on the path where Owen had left her. And then as he watched she turned all around, a complete circle. It was as if she was looking for somebody who ought to be there, but wasn't.

Owen watched her.

Good, he thought. *Good.*

When the alarm went off at 4 the next morning, Owen was already awake, staring into the dark. He had a headache that seemed to extend down one arm to his elbow, and something else as well—a knowledge in his bones—that made him feel heavy, swollen. But he got up and dressed in the dark of the house and then he went out into the dark outside. When he had hitched up his team, he climbed onto the rack and started out.

It wasn't like an ordinary year. The sound of wagons in the dark: ordinarily that was a sound to put life into a man. But this year it was only hard wheels on hard road, and the sound of his pitchfork bump, bump, bumping on the bare floor of the rack. Owen didn't think about what might be coming. He didn't tell himself that this job was better than no job. He wasn't speaking to himself at all.

There were a dozen men sitting in the yellow light of the lamp when he got to the Allsopps, all of them forking up beef and potatoes. There were three strangers among them: Staunton, Elreno and a young fellow from Ontario, a boy who had been drifting through when Staunton hired him. The rest of the men, all of whom had worked together before, were trying to bridge their feeling of strangeness with the newcomers by joking.

Owen didn't join in. He didn't feel like eating but he ate; he had to if he wanted to work. As he ate, he took a good look at Staunton's son.

Elreno didn't look the way he would have expected him to look. Staunton was big-bellied and Elreno was lean. Staunton had that strange, gentle voice; Elreno showed signs of being a loudmouth. But the most surprising thing was that Elreno had a moustache. Owen noticed that there were no jokes about Elreno's moustache. Nobody suggested that they would all gang up on him in the bunkhouse some night and shave it off.

"Last year I was second-in-command," Elreno announced. "But this year I'm running the show." He wasn't joking exactly; he wanted them to know.

The big push, Owen thought. That was what the men would be calling Elreno in a few days.

He could see the other men sizing the Stauntons up and coming to their own conclusions. Like Owen, not too many of them had much to be concerned about as far as knowing their jobs went. Do your job right and there was nothing anybody could bawl you out about. Owen had been threshing for ten years and he'd never been bawled out yet. He never expected to be.

Pretty soon they finished eating. "Time to start, boys," Staunton said. But then he remembered that Elreno was the boss now. He turned to Elreno to let him give the orders.

"You, Blackie," Elreno said. He was looking at Owen. "You and Stevenson can start out now. You can be first up. And Deacon and Sedgewick can follow you."

It was the first time in his life that anyone had ever called

Owen *Blackie.* Before he could decide how he felt about it, Staunton spoke again. "I've never had a black working for me before," he said.

The men laughed, nervously. Owen didn't join in. He pushed himself back from the table and turned to young Bob Allsopp, who was field-pitching. "Want a ride out?" he asked.

They went into the yard then: Owen, Stevenson and Bob Allsopp. But as Owen was untying his lines, Staunton appeared at the side of his rack.

"Look," Staunton said, "I guess I shouldn't have said what I did just now."

In the gathering light, Owen saw that he looked like he meant it. "I was only making fun," Staunton said.

Owen nodded, acknowledging the apology.

Then, "Another thing," Staunton said. "I'd take it as a favour if you'd drive my team for a day or two."

For a minute, Owen didn't say anything. If he was driving Staunton's team, that meant that the young fellow from Ontario would be driving his. It was a lot to ask a man: to put his team into the hands of a boy he didn't even know.

He hesitated a moment, considering. There was the clatter of an empty rack as Stevenson started off for the field.

"It's not that my team's not broke," Staunton said. "We had them threshing last year. But the little mare never did get over being nervous around the separator. It would be better for the first few days if she had a good man driving her."

He was asking Owen as an older man, a man who knew horses, to give the boy a break. There was no way Owen could refuse.

"I'll give it a try," Owen said.

"I appreciate that," Staunton said.

So Owen tied his lines and climbed off his own rack and on to Staunton's. Staunton followed him, stopping to pat the mare on her rump. "She's a good little horse," he said. "I've never had one I liked better."

With the Allsopp boy beside him, Owen started off for the field. When he got there he headed for the south fence. Owen liked to go to the far side of a field and then work in toward the machine.

It was easy work: pitching the bundles up. The crop was thin and light and the bundles were small: about a third of the size a bundle ought to be. But the stooks were so far apart that you had a lot of walking to do. Besides that, there was a lot of loose stuff that the binder had missed. It took a long time to make a load.

Going in, Owen heard the outfit before he saw it. He came over a hill with his load and saw Staunton and Elreno standing together in front of the separator, identical sweater collars pulled high out of identical combination overalls. Stevenson was already in, pitching in bundles on the north side of the feeder.

The beginning of a straw pile was forming underneath the blower, and the first wheat formed a russet arc from grain spout to waggon box. Chaff hung suspended in the stillness of the morning. Seeing it, Owen felt the rhythm of the season reaching out to him. He wanted to get his team in there, to start pitching bundle for bundle with Stevenson.

He headed Staunton's horses in and their heads went down and their ears went back. As they got closer to the noise and the dust and the long flapping belts, the little mare began to shake. Owen saw that she was the kind of horse that would shake like this every time she was brought in, all the time he was unloading. But he had no difficulty driving her in to where she was supposed to go. It was as if she had forgotten there was any alternative.

Owen tied his lines to the linepost before he picked up his fork. He wouldn't have bothered with his own team but this team was different. He didn't trust them. And tied, they couldn't run away. They couldn't pull a waggon with their mouths.

When they were tied, he began to pitch down his load. It was rhythmic work, keeping the feeder loaded. The bundles, once they were on the feeder, didn't remain bundles very long. Chains glittered and slats rattled and the bundles jiggled up to the twine cutter. Then the curved steel blades came down and the bundles collapsed and disappeared into the cylinder.

The second load took even longer to pick up than the first, because he picked up most of it alone. Bob Allsopp was off helping another man.

When he pulled in to the machine, Staunton was gone, but Elreno was there, waiting for him. Again, the machine was running empty on his side when he came in.

Owen tied his lines. As he started to unload, Elreno walked back from the tractor. He raised his voice so that Owen could hear him over the noise of the machinery.

"Just where in hell do you think you've been?" he demanded.

Owen looked at him, but he didn't answer. There was no answer to a question like that. But as he pitched bundles his resentment grew. Elreno knew how light the crop was this year. He knew how far you had to walk to get a load. And if he didn't know how much loose stuff there was to be picked up, he ought to know. Did he want you to leave the loose stuff in the field? That would give him something to holler about, wouldn't it?

But Owen knew that Elreno hadn't hollered because he was late. Elreno hollered because he believed that hollering was his right. Or else because he wanted to show everybody right from the start who was boss.

As Owen forked the last of his load onto the feeder, he saw that Frank Deacon had pulled into place behind him. And then he saw Elreno walking up to Deacon. Elreno stood beneath Deacon's rack, looking up.

"I suppose you call that a load?" he said.

Frank Deacon didn't bother to deny that his load was light. It wasn't, and Elreno knew it.

Deacon looped his lines over the linepost, climbed down the front of the rack, and faced Elreno.

"Listen, Elreno," he said. "I'm willing to settle this here and now. Find out which one of us is the better man."

Frank Deacon was a well-built man, and handy with his fists. Elreno looked at him for a minute. Then he tried to look disdainful. But then he turned and started walking back to the machine.

Looking around, Owen saw the men exchanging smiles. *Elreno went back a lot faster than he come out,* they would say later. *And a good job he did,* they would say. *Frank Deacon don't back down from nobody.*

Suddenly Owen felt again the shame there was in being small. A man ought to be big, like Frank Deacon. A man ought not to put up with things. He had put up with things, had kept his trap shut while Elreno gave him hell. He had let Staunton come into his house, had let Staunton hold his child. It seemed to Owen that Staunton and Elreno weren't really two different people at all; they were one and the same. As he and Estelle were one and the same, or had been one and the same.

But when Owen thought of Estelle, the way he thought of her was as she had been on Staunton's knee: sitting quietly while Staunton pawed over her. And when he thought that, something new happened to Owen. His thoughts stopped altogether and a feeling came over him. It came over him in waves, wave on wave of it, as if it had started a long way back and built up until now it was irresistible; it had to be surrendered to.

He swung his lines, startling Staunton's team. They took off at a trot. The rack rattled and the pitchfork bumped on the bare floor, but Owen didn't hear them. He didn't think either: not about himself and Estelle, or Staunton and Elreno. It was as if he had left them all behind, himself included, back at the separator. He did not think about what had happened as he drove away to the north side of the field, beyond the place where he would encounter field pitchers or other teams. He didn't think about anything at all. He just drove the team until he had got away, behind a hill where he wouldn't see anybody, and nobody would see him.

He tied his lines. He couldn't do anything with his lines, not what needed to be done. He took a long time tying them, as if he were moving in sleep. It was very important that he do it right.

When he had finished, he moved to the back of the rack and picked up his fork. He got off the rack and went up to the team. And then he began to beat them.

Them... it. It was the mare's side he had come up on, and so she was the one that got it. She leapt and twisted in her harness. Beadings of blood appeared on her haunches and thighs. And then strings of blood swung in the air, red and viscous, as she twisted, trying to escape him. But he didn't let her. He didn't stop beating her until he was too tired to go on. And then he sat on the ground, and put his head on his knees, and wept.

It was a long time before he began to wonder how he would explain the blood on the mare to Mr. Staunton.